ABANDONED

ABANDONED

KIAN SABIK

GLOSSARY

Bèndàn - Idiot

Dìdì - Younger Brother

Dopa - A traditional Uyghur hat

Gǒu - Dog

Háizi - Child

Móguǐ - Devil

Núlì - Slaves

Qiúfàn - Prisoners

Pàntú - Traitor

Xíngshì - Brat

Yě shòu - Beast

Yěmán rén - Barbarians

Zuìfàn - Criminal

Please note that the words under the chapter numbers are numbers in the Uyghur language

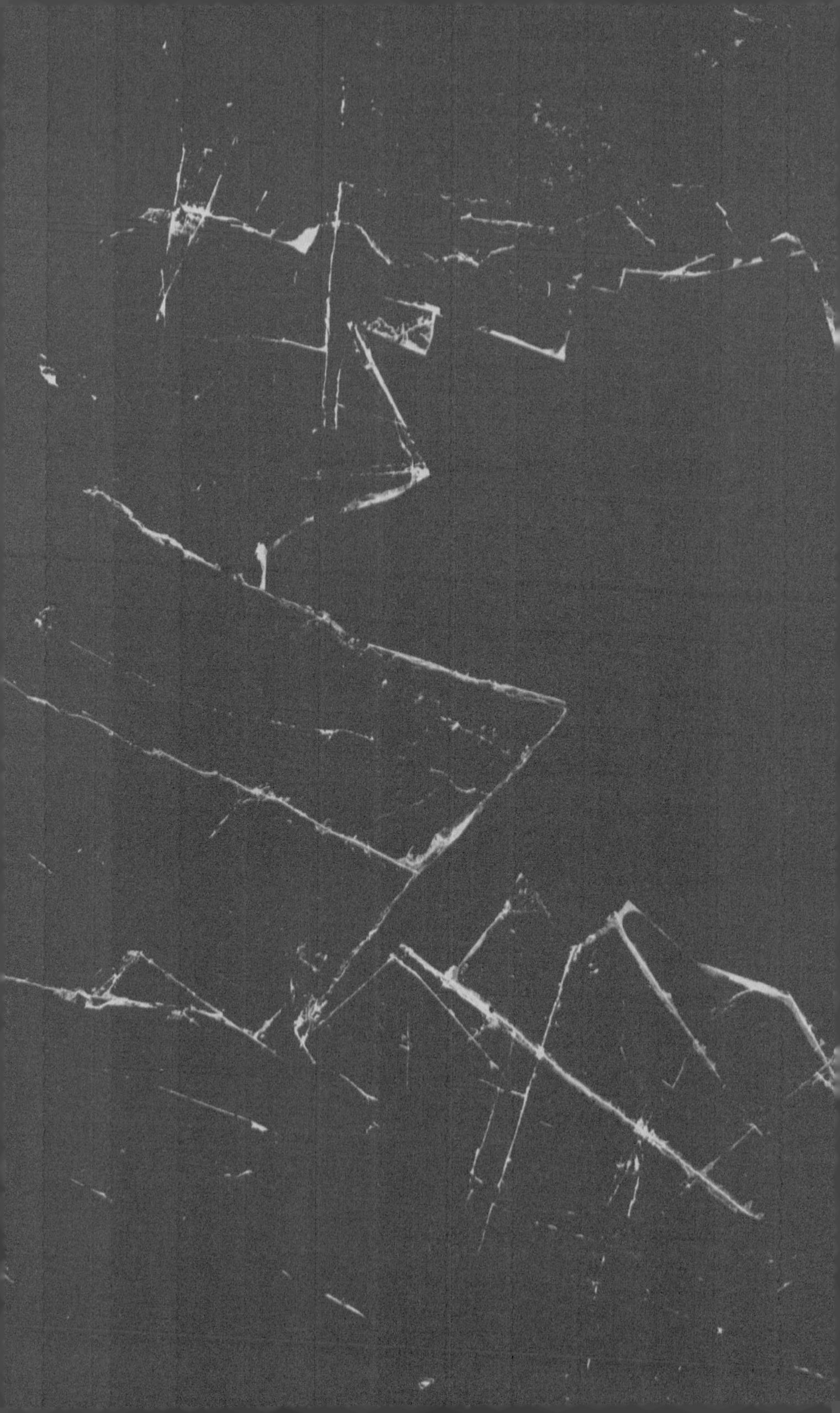

HALA
KAZAKHSTAN
NOW

1

BIR

THE CACKLING INK whispers back at me.

You're Next

The words warp into a spiral, drawing my eyes closer and closer. I jerk my head backward and dig my fingers into my hair.

Everything was going so well. Life was finally *livable.* We were supposed to leave. We were supposed to be far away from China.

My breath grows shallow, in synchrony with my throbbing mind.

Mama has disappeared. Papa is dead. Ürkesh is missing. I'm the only one left.

And now,

They're

Coming

After

Me.

I look up from my feet to the barren street. A few white clouds dot the sky and the sun's beams warm everything they touch.

Except for me.

My teeth clang together and I rub my arms. A dark figure approaches from the corner of my eye. I straighten my back and turn to my right but no one is there.

Now you're paranoid.

I scan the bright street but the figure is nowhere to be found. A flash of movement catches my eye.

A deep, fluttery feeling settles into my stomach.

Thump. Thump.

I glance around the area one last time, trying to keep my panic at bay.

But it doesn't work. I inch backward.

Crash.

I slam the apartment gate shut.

Thud. Thud.

I dart up the endless stairs, glancing back over my shoulder. I shut the front door closed.

Abandoned

Click. Click.

I fasten every lock I can get my hands on and sink into the wall behind me. Taking in shallow breaths, I try to calm my racing mind.

Bang. Bang.

I jump away from the door.

Bang. Bang. Bang.

The door creaks from the center as I back up further. My heart pounds against my chest.

I need to think straight. I need to have a clear mind.

I step into Mama's room and try to process everything.

There aren't many places to hide. The only way to escape is through the window.

Bang. Bang.

The pounding from the front pushes me forward. I peer out the window. The ground is

So

Far

Away

My breathing gets heavier and heavier.

You need to find something to fight with.

I jump toward the wooden side tables, slide open the drawers and rummage through their contents.

Socks, a book, letters, *a phone.*

I stash the phone into the pocket inside my shirt. As I slide it in, something hard glides against my fingers. I take out a small knife and glare at it. A set of dark, terrified eyes look back at me.

My eyes.

You should have remembered that you had this. You kept it near you for emergencies.

I shudder. The thought of blood sends shivers down my spine.

Crash.

A deafening sound echoes throughout the small apartment. Heavy footsteps rush through the house. I take a deep breath and dive under the wooden bed, stuffing myself between a few blankets. I bury my face into the cotton.

A storm erupts.

Dishes shatter.

Glass explodes.

Walls rumble.

The menacing footsteps grow louder and louder.

I cover my ears to block the noise out but the muffled crashing still rings in my ears. I squeeze harder and harder until...silence.

Deathly, screaming silence.

I slowly take my hands off my ears and listen. The pounding from earlier continues ringing in my ears. My muscles tense and something flutters in my stomach.

Something's not right.

...

Whoosh.

A hand claws at my ankle and the floor disappears from beneath me. I grip the blankets but they are no use against the force pulling me out. A hand shoves them over my face, blinding me. My breath grows warm and shallow.

I punch, kick, scratch and scream.

But nothing happens.

I try feeling for my knife but it's not in my hands anymore.

Whoosh. Crash.

Air rushes out of my lungs as my neck cracks from the impact. I hiss and my limbs go limp.

Do something...anything...just...

A lone tear streams down my cheek.

This is where it ends.

The blankets covering my face fall to my feet as a towering figure grows crisp. His head is barely covered by black hair. Dark shadows circle his hollow, rough eyes and a long greenish-purple streak is painted on his face. His lips form a tight frown, revealing black gaps among the white when it opens.

My jaw drops and I blink rapidly.

"Ürkesh? *Ürkesh? What are you doing?*" I shriek.

His frown turns into a scowl and his eyes catch on fire. "You thought you could run around freely after betraying your country? Did you seriously underestimate us that much?" he spits out.

"Wha...what? Ürkesh? What happened to you?"

He pulls me away from the wall and

crash,

slams me back into it.

"Ürkesh?"

Crash.

"I don't think you understood. Keep your mouth *shut."*

A white flash comes out from behind him. Before I have a chance to yelp, a damp cloth is slapped onto my mouth.

I thrash,

I punch,

I kick,

Until my mind drifts off as everything around me begins to sway.

D   A   R   K   N   E   S   S

2

IKKI

W   A   S

      T   I

   H   T   I

            H   S

Mmmhhh.

My eyes flutter open to black. It's as if the Earth is balanced on top of my head.

I don't know if I'm right-side up or not. I don't know where I am. I try to open my mouth but *krrrr,* the tape just crinkles. I try my wrists but they're chained together.

Screech.

Smash.

I lurch forward, hitting something hard. The realization drips in.

I'm in a vehicle.

They're taking me back,

Back to the camp,

Back to the cell,

Back to the prison.

I open my eyes to find a sliver of light tearing through the darkness from beneath my chin. I shake my head vigorously, the cloth finally slipping off.

I take a breath of the fresh, cool air. Warm light tickles my eyes.

Then chaos strikes. Darkness creeps through the trunk until it swallows everything around me.

Mama's disappearance. The break in. Ürkesh. Passing out.

The fuzz grows larger and heavier until it sinks into my body.

Then I see it.

A chiseled corner juts out from the crate in front of me. I scoot forward until my wrists align with the scarped corner. I take a deep breath, shut my eyes and begin rubbing my skin against it.

Rubbing,

rubbing,

and rubbing,

Until it feels like a fire has ignited on my flesh.

I can't stop. I can't stop until the ropes are off.

I

Need

To

Get

Out

Of

Here.

Screech.

Before the last few fibers are torn, the vehicle lurches forward and I tumble to the back of the trunk.

Thud. Thud.

    Thud. Thud.

        THUD. THUD.

        THUD. THUD.

Krrr.

The trunk door slides open and light floods into the car.

Shhhrrrr.

I shut my eyes closed and pretend to go limp. Rough, clumsy hands slide the crates around until the fort surrounding me has been demolished.

"I see you followed my orders," a deep voice booms.

"Yes, Father. I would never disobey you."

Ürkesh? *Father?* What is going on?

An icy hand squeezes my wrist. "Hm, she's alive. If she wasn't, I would have peeled your skin off."

Ürkesh doesn't respond. The man gripping my wrist sighs, his breath gliding over my skin.

"Wake up, *Gǒu*," the voice commands. My mind is too numb to understand. The words

go in one ear   and out the other.

"I'm talking to you, girl. I know you're awake. You can't deceive me that easily. Who do you think I am?" The man's voice grows sharp and thin.

Fear seizes my heart.

The ground disappears from beneath my back and my arm jerks back and forth,

But my eyes still won't open.

Because I'm afraid.

I'm afraid of what I'll see.

I'm afraid of the pain.

I'm afraid of the fear.

"*Xíngshì*, you can't fool me. You should know better." I can hear the man's smirk through his voice. "I shouldn't need to describe what happens to the disobedient, right?"

Aaaaaah.

The sharp shrieks of the eaten man ring in my ears. The dog chewing at his face. The red river flowing from his flesh. His crimson bones.

I shudder and peel my eyes open. Two fuzzy blobs grow crisp. One looms over me, his hand gripping my wrist. A deep, clean scar runs across his face and his hair is combed back neatly. His skin is almost spotless with only a few blemishes near his sharp nose. The man...*looks* like Ürkesh.

Thump. Thump. Thump.

My blood freezes when I see the boy next to him.

The boy with empty eyes.

A permanent scowl.

A rock-hard face.

The boy I once knew as my brother.

But now, I know as a stranger.

"Ürkesh," I whisper.

"That's not my name," he says, gritting his teeth, "My name is Kai. Fu Kai."

"No, that's not your name. You're Ürkesh. My brother."

The man holding me steps besides Ürkesh. "He's not your brother and he never has been. He's *my* son," he says.

Chen.

The realization slams into me.

The man is Chen.

The man Mama was afraid of.

"It's about time I got to meet Lin's daughter. I've heard so much about you from Bao. It seems he wasn't able to keep your rebellious tendencies in check. You even managed to escape the country for a few days. But no one gets away from *me*. The question is how did you get out?"

The words clump in my throat.

"Bao told me you were...fiery and sharp, not quiet. It seems like you've *changed*. Are you afraid, little girl?" Chen mocks, his face getting closer and closer to mine.

Don't show him your fear. You can't let him get to you.

"Tell me, how did you get out of China?" Chen asks again, a hit of steel woven in his voice.

I barely shake my head.

"Don't say no to me. How did you escape China?"

"I don't know," I whisper, my eyes glued to the stone floor.

He sighs and rubs the bridge of his nose. "That doesn't matter to me right now. I will get the answer from you sooner or later," he takes a brief pause, "Now, I want you to meet someone very *special* to me. Someone I hadn't seen in years. Follow me."

A boulder settles in my throat but I follow Chen to a building across the camp. The gloomy sky around it hides the sun's warmth as the clouds grow darker. They strangle the building, its silent screams echoing in my ear. The crushed, dry dirt grips my feet, holding them down.

I peer side to side, the monotonous gray spread across the horizon. The echoing sound of machines, the sound of screams, ring in my ears. Spots of red are scattered on the ground.

Thumpthump. Thumpthump.

Chen grips a door handle and pulls it open, revealing the black inside. A familiar stench hits me.

The stench of death,

pain,

and terror.

My stomach sinks.

I'm back in a camp.

I'm back in a prison.

I'm back *here*.

"Are you coming or what?" Chen yells from afar.

"I'm sorry, sir," I mutter and start down the murky hall.

Eerie footsteps echo throughout the hallway and the sounds of tears ring in every corner.

Whoosh.

A sudden flash of movement rushes past me. An icy hand tears at my legs and a muffled shriek slips from my mouth.

"I haven't done anything wrong. Please let me out of here. I just want to see children again," a shadowy woman cries, pulling me close until the cool metal bars rest against my face.

Cling.

I smash into the cell door but the woman continues tugging.

"Please, please, *please*," she begins to scream, her voice growing hoarse, *"Please. Please. Please."*

"But...I...what...I," My tongue trembles and my voice crackles.

I can't say no.

I can't.

I can't.

I can't say anything.

Crack.

The woman's pleas plummet down a cliff, only the muffled *drip* of her tears ringing.

I back away from the cell door, my breath growing heavy.

Nothing moves.

The woman stays in her place, the black still blanketing her.

Splash.

My foot sinks in a thick puddle. I peel my foot away and the smell hits me.

Blood.

The puddle is of blood.

The lights flicker on, illuminating the entire passageway. The stick-like woman grips a bar of the door. Her face is a ghostly white and her hand dangles lifelessly, a river of red flowing out of it.

"Please," she whispers and she begins to weep.

I force my eyes away, my breath growing heavier with each blink. I lift my heavy foot to take a step when my eyes meet his.

Chen leans against a wall, his hand around a metal pipe smeared with blood.

"Come on. You don't want to miss the *surprise*, do you?"

I force my feet to move and a sickening feeling bubbles in my stomach.

This man is worse than Bao.

The flashing lightbulbs fly by as I drag myself. Chen's footsteps are within earshot but his shadow is the only thing I can see. The darkness in the corners awakens and growls as I pass by.

And then, there's silence.

Deathly silence.

Chen stands near a cell, gazing down. His eyes remain locked on something but his face is empty of emotion.

"Come closer," he commands and suddenly, his eyes turn red.

I step forward and peer into the cell. A lone, crumpled figure lies there, her hands shielding her face. Soft whimpers and sharp cries come from her and she trembles violently. Her hair is torn in patches with deep cuts painted on her skin.

No.

A whimper escapes my lips.

The seconds pass by like hours.

The woman slowly removes her hands and her gaze locks with mine.

Her eyes widen.

Her mouth hangs loose.

And the sheer look of terror is glued onto her face.

Heavy tears stream down her face and she shakes her head in disbelief.

And lies there.

Staring and sobbing.

"Mama," I whisper.

She forces her eyes away and her tears echo throughout the hall. My breath grows shallow.

I try to move away but my feet are glued to the ground.

A hand jerks me backward.

"Do you like my surprise?" Chen says, savoring my shock.

A brick lodges in my throat.

"Now, I need you to understand one very simple rule. If you misbehave, you *and* your mother are going to die. Understand?"

I nod vigorously.

"Good. Go to Kai. He will give you further instructions."

"Yes, sir," I whisper, my eyes locked with the stone floor.

I trudge back down the hallway, my heart still stuck at Mama's cell. My feet carry themselves down the hallway as if I already know where to go.

Nǐmen dūhuì sǐ de.

I skid to a stop and turn my head to face the words. A tiny gasp escapes from my lungs.

You all are going to die.

A blizzard whirls in my bones. I can't move. My feet glue themselves to the ground.

"What are you reading?" A figure steps out from the shadows.

"Ürkesh—"

"Don't. My name is *not* Ürkesh. It's Kai. Father is right about you all," he mutters under his breath.

"Urke...Kai, please. I'm your sister."

"You are *not* my sister. You wouldn't be chained up in this place then."

"Don't you remember who I am? Who *you* are?" I plead.

"There is nothing to remember. You *Uyghurs* are in this place because of your revolts. You all are too...rebellious. We need to get rid of all threats to our security. That's all that matters. China and my father are the only people that matter," he responds coldly.

"Chen is *not* a real father. A real father wouldn't be like...like *him.*"

Ürkesh's eyes turn red. "How *dare* you say these things about Father. You don't even know the first thing about him. *You Núli don't know anything,"* he yells.

"Can you even hear yourself? What is wrong with you?" I spit out without thinking.

Crack.

An arm swings from nowhere, lighting my face on fire.

Thump. Thump. Thump.

My heartbeat rings in my ears.

Ürkesh just slapped me.

My brother just slapped me.

My brother, who I love so much.

But now,

He doesn't have a speck of compassion for me.

What has Chen done?

The tears flood out and I can't stop them. They drip down my face, drenching my clothes. Ürkesh just stands there, watching my tears splash against the floor. "You're not a child. Time to get to work."

He shoves me forward and my feet turn into water. The world spins and plummets as my head meets the stone floor.

"Get up."

Ürkesh's foot meets my stomach and I gag.

"You'll get much more if you don't get up *right now.*"

I peer into Ürkesh's eyes. His empty, cold eyes. And I search.

But there's nothing left to find.

I heave myself up and walk into the darkness, Ürkesh's looming presence right behind me.

3

ÜCH

A LARGE DOOR slams behind me and Ürkesh shoves me deeper into the room.

Memories rush to me.

Memories of an unforgettable past.

Memories of Bao.

Memories of Uncle Shan.

And now this.

I examine my surroundings but no one dares to look into my eyes. Only a few children shift their heads.

A weight rests on my shoulder and I freeze. "Not here. *There.*"

A rough force guides me to a small, camouflaged door. I swim through the sea of workers and they part, shuffling as far away as they can.

Creeeeeak.

The door screeches open and rays of sunlight tickle my face. I shield my eyes from the blinding light and take in the scene.

White buds sprout from green sticks. The clouds dot the sky and the wind races through the field, laughing. My bare feet melt in the soft, dark soil and I soak in the warmth.

A thought slams into me.

The whole world is continuing on as if nothing is happening. Everyone is continuing on without us. They've left us behind.

No one cares.

Instantly, the white melts into black and the warmth into a chilly wind.

Someone shoves a scratchy bag into my hands. "Start collecting and *don't stop.*"

"Ürkesh, please."

"Stop calling me Ürkesh. That's not my name. I'm Kai, son of the honorable Chen," he barks.

"Yes, sir," I whisper.

"That's more like it. Now, get to work."

I step into the plants but my feet refuse to move any further. They sink deeper and deeper into the soil. My breath becomes shallow and my head spins. The green buds around me merge into a wave, growing and growing until it swallows me whole. I'm left in a black void,

Where I can't see

I can't hear

I can't feel

Where there's just

B   L   A   C   K

Crack.

White pain erupts from my back and a fire eats at my bones.

"Get. To. Work," Ürkesh bellows, a whip laughing in his hands.

I nod, my eyes glued to the ground and I rip out the white fluffs. More of them stick to my fingers than go into the bag and soon, my hands look like clouds.

I wish I could be a cloud, floating peacefully, not feeling pain. I wish my hands could become clouds and take me up with them.

I close my eyes and think of happiness.

Of laughter.

Of warmth.

But I can't.

Only pain,

Sadness,

And ice come to mind.

When I try to think of the Ürkesh I knew, Chen's face replaces it.

I glance up to catch Ürkesh's gaze on me. My fingers rip the cotton out of the shoots but my eyes remain fixed on his.

Maybe...just maybe, he will come back.

His face hardens and his lips tighten into a scowl. The fire in his eyes burns brighter, burning the little hope I had inside.

"It seems you're not focused on your work."

I stifle a yelp. The voice comes close to my ear. "Your mother's life is hanging by a thread. You get to decide when the scissor cuts it. If you won't be a good girl, *snip*, your mother is gone," Chen's fingers snip in front of me.

"Yes, sir," I whisper, my voice slightly shaking.

"Good. I see we understand each other perfectly. It's as if you really are my blood."

A storm runs down my spine.

Thud.

Wind rushes out of my lungs and the rustle of leaves embraces me. A sharp pain emerges from my skull and I lie in the cotton plants for a few seconds, trying to understand what just happened.

"I never knew little girls were so weak. You touch them and they fall," Chen chuckles and his footsteps disappear.

I lift myself off the ground and place my red fingers in my mouth.

There's no room for feelings here.

THE DAY is finally over.

I lie on the icy floor, surrounded by nothing but silence.

"It's best you remain isolated from the other prisoners in case you give them some ideas," *Chen says, a smirk plastered on his face. "If you behave, I might let you sleep in a different cell. But so far, you haven't impressed me."*

"I will try my best, sir," I respond, a little louder this time.

"That's what I want to hear," He turns toward the guard. "You know what you should do."

"Yes, sir." The man salutes Chen as he disappears into the darkness.

The man turns toward me with chains in his hands, his eyes scanning the area. "Please forgive me."

I try to turn but my hands burn against the stone floor. My arms are stretched downward, clamped to my ankles.

I can't move at all.

I force my eyes upward to gaze through the tiny window. The moon is still ruling outside and the stars burn brightly. They're so far away from here. So far away from the darkness.

I close my eyes and think of life before all this. Before the government took everything.

But I can't. I can hardly remember any of it.

I glance to my side, at the wide pot beside me. It's slightly raised from the phone underneath.

Chen better not do cell inspections.

Muffled tears drip in the cell next to mine and gentle sobs echo throughout the hallway. I drag myself to the opposite wall and place my ear on the cold surface, taking in Mama's tears.

"It's okay, Mama. We'll be fine. We'll all be fine," I whisper, my breath turning into white fog.

I wish she could hear that.

I wish she could know that I can hear her tears.

I wish she could know that she should be stronger.

For me.

I jolt awake at the *thud* of boots. I scramble to get up before being pulled back down. I try again but the metal wrapped around me jerks me back.

Click.

The thick door *creaks* open to reveal the guard from yesterday. He steps toward me, the key swinging in his hand.

He reaches for the lock and *clink,* the metal snaps open, freeing my wrists and ankles. I rub my angry skin and nod at the kind stranger.

He goes back to the door and stands there. "Is she out yet?" Chen yells, his voice sharp like a distant bolt of lightning.

"Yes, sir," the guard calls out and gestures me over. "Where should she go?"

"Back to the cotton field. I don't have enough people over there."

As the guard takes me to the fields, he stops at a deep, undisturbed corner. The shadows cover most of it and a lone chair resides, rusted blood painted on it. A small barrier runs around it, shards of glass scattered on the dull floor. A frame hangs on the wall.

I gaze at the young boy, his smile spread across the picture. He's a little older than me and his deep eyes give a peek into his personality. He looks like a kind, courageous boy.

He reminds me of Ürkesh.

I warp back into reality. The guard continues staring at the picture, his frown growing bigger as tears pool in eyes. After a few seconds, he rips his eyes away and heads deeper into the hallway.

"Come on," he commands softly while swallowing his emotions. His rigid face returns after a few seconds. "You don't want to cross Chen. Please, please, don't make him angry," he begs.

"Yes. Of course," I respond and smile slightly, even though the both of us are holding back our tears.

He returns the smile before the door slams shut.

I pick up a scratchy sack and trudge down the rows of green and white.

It's the same scene as yesterday.

Before my hands meet the cotton, a figure walks to my side and stops. I turn to find a young girl, about my age, staring at me. Her hair is longer than anyone else's, knotted in braids, and her head reaches until my nose. Her clothes ruffle with the wind and pool around her wrists and ankles. The skin on her wrist is puffy, the word *Gǒu* burned onto it.

She drops her eyes. She shakes her head, her eyes glued to the ground. After a few moments, she finally rips them away but as soon as she looks at me, the tears flood in.

"It's all my fault...it's all my fault...Kai-Kai-" she stutters.

"What?"

4

TÖT

"KAI?"

The girl's eyes bulge out of their sockets. "You're Hala," she whispers.

?　　　　　?　　　　?　　　　　　　?
　　　?　　　?　　　　?
　?　　　　?　　?　　?　　?

My heart beats wildly.
"How do you know?"
"You…you look like Kai and you—"
"How do *you* know Kai?"
Shadows swallow her eyes.

"He was a prisoner here before...*this* happened. I... Mei...My name is Mei. I knew him. He mentioned you a lot. But I don't know what Chen did to him. I don't know what happened. But now, he's just...different..."

An eerie silence sinks down.

Thump. Thump. Thump. Thump.

Ürkesh was here.

He was fine before. Something happened.

Chen did something.

My voice cracks. "Tell me about him. Tell me what happened here."

Mei nods, takes a deep breath and gazes at the ground. "Chen was very focused on your brother. Kai tried to escape over three times and it got him in a lot of trouble. He was punished severely in every way possible. He changed after his friend...his friend..."

She doesn't need to complete the rest. A brick lodges into my heart, causing it to sink into the depths of my stomach.

Yu is dead.

"He wasn't the same afterward. He was constantly getting in trouble. Constantly escaping. The last time I saw him, he was locked up. Chen was making him humiliate himself in front of everyone. But he didn't. He didn't because..."

Mei looks down to her feet. "I begged him not to say those things. I begged him to motivate us all. After he did that, he…he disappeared. He came back a week ago but he's not the same."

ThumpThump. ThumpThump.

My mind goes numb.

I can't see anything.

I can hear anything.

All I can feel is red.

Angry, boiling red.

Grrrrrrrrrrrrrr.

I want to fight Chen.

I want to punch him,

I want to kick him,

I want to bite him,

I want him to feel

   Every

      Single

         Nightmare

he dragged me into.

Every nightmare he dragged *Ürkesh* into.

THUMPTHUMP.

   THUMPTHUMP.

      THUMPTHUMP.

         THUMPTHUMP.

Stop. You need to calm down. Anger won't help. You need to calm down.

   THUMPTHUMP.

      ThumpThump.

        Thump.

Thump.

I sink back into reality and the sound of tears is the first thing I hear.

"It's all my fault. He's gone because of me. He was punished because of—"

"*Shhh.*" I place my hand on her shoulder and squeeze gently. "None of this is your fault."

I wrap my arms around her and let her drench my shirt.

"They're all gone because of me," her voice comes out muffled from deep within me, "Everyone is gone because of me. I didn't want to work. I didn't understand the situation back then. I should have listened to my mom. I should have listened. But I didn't. I didn't and Chen killed them *all*. Even my baby sister. She was only a few months old. She's gone...all of them are gone because of *me*."

"None of this is your fault, Mei. None of it. You need to understand that. You are not guilty," I try to comfort her but her sobs only get deeper.

I hold onto her a little longer until her tears dry up. She peels off me and gazes at the ground, digging her feet into the dirt.

"I'm sorry...about that," she murmurs shamefully.

"No, no. We're all here for each other." I smile at her and she slightly returns it.

"Get back to work."

Both of us stiffen at the command and our arms start moving, ripping cotton off the stalks.

Fast, light footsteps approach us and a large shadow reigns over us. I freeze at the sound of the figure breathing but Mei continues as if nothing is happening.

"Never forget, your lives are in my hands," Chen whispers in my ear, "It would be a shame to see your mother dead, right?"

A vision flashes before my eyes. Mama drowning in a sea of dark, fresh blood. Her eyes are lifeless and a deep, black wound separates her neck and body.

I can smell the heavy stench of death.

I can feel the crimson liquid flowing past my feet.

I can hear the fatal, agonizing silence.

Crack.

A bolt of lightning flashes from the sky. I whip around to stare into Chen's devilish eyes. I don't dare reach for my numb face and bite my tongue.

Control yourself. Control yourself.

I swallow my stinging tears and keep myself from ripping his eyes out.

Chen grins. "Next time, pay attention."

He gets up and strolls back to the shade.

I don't move until he's swallowed by the towering building. A deep breath escapes my burning lungs and I reach for my face. My cheek tingles as my fingers brush against it. I glance over at Mei and she nods, a steely mask plastered on her face. She raises a finger to her lips.

Shhh.

Ddddddeeeee. Ddddddeeee.

A sharp ringing pierces the tense air and a wave of people flood into a building. Mei and I are swept into it and we wash up in a large, empty room. The stench of rotten bread punches my nose and bile climbs my throat.

You have to eat if you want to survive.

I help Mei off the ground and we squeeze into the line. As I hold my plate out, a thick, murky goop is scooped onto it and a piece of blue bread is thrown at me. A small, stained cup of water is shoved into my hands and that's it. That's all we get to eat for the entire day.

My stomach gurgles at the sight of the supposed food.

You've got to eat with your mouth, not your eyes.

I take a deep breath and throw the contents of the plate down my throat. I force it down, keeping the vomit from spraying out of my mouth.

Grrrrrrrrrrrrr.

I press my hand against my stomach but it continues gurgling, begging for some decent food.

My mind flutters to the last meal I remember having at home.

Me, Ürkesh, Mama and Papa laughing on the floor, water shooting out of our noses. Ürkesh falls over, gripping his stomach, laughing hysterically. Mama and Papa glance at each other and their faces light up.

I warp back into reality. I look around at the other prisoners. Some faces I recognize from our neighborhood. They were once bright, laughing faces.

Now, they look like ghosts of their past.

They are sticks in clothes, their skin clinging to their bones and their eyes are lifeless. They are corpses.

Hollow,

Frozen

Corpses.

Their mouths are glued into frowns and dark circles are painted under their eyes. Wrinkles spread on their faces while their heads remain bare except for a few, lone strands of hair.

A hand grips my shoulder and forces me back into reality. I gaze into Mei's eyes and she shakes her head.

"Don't," she mouths and her eyes dart toward the guards chuckling at the doors.

I nod and close my eyes to prevent myself from searching the room.

Ddddeeeee.

Everyone gets up and forms a river, its multiple branches flowing into different areas of the camp. My feet float through the room until suddenly, they freeze.

The cotton fields.

I can't go. I can't go back. Not now.

I grip Mei's wrist and dash into a dark corner.

"What are you doing?" she whisper-yells, her eyes bulging out.

"I...I need a minute. I can't go back into the fields. Let's just stay here."

"No, I'm not risking our lives. Come on, we're going to where we're *supposed* to be."

"You can go. I'm staying here for a while."

"Please. Come on. I can't let them kill you too," Mei begs.

"No. Give me a few minutes and I'll come." I gently push her back into the crowd. She glances back at me with heavy eyes and disappears.

I squeeze myself deeper into the corner and inhale deep breaths.

Get a hold of yourself. You have to—

Scccreeeeeeech.

A sharp noise pierces through the air. I cover my ears tightly, trying to block out the sound.

Silence.

What was that?

I peer from side to side and walk into the dark hallway beside me. Hushed hisses spray warm air into my face but otherwise, there is complete silence.

Sccccreeeech.

I grip my ears and shut my eyes, waiting for the noise to leave. A sigh of relief exits my lungs once the quiet settles back in.

A shallow stream of light comes from the end of the hallway. I press myself against the wall and tip-toe there, freezing with every sound.

A door.

There's light coming from the door.

I peer into the door. Machines pant and people hurl commands at each other.

I place my head against the wall. Something bumpy rests against my skull. I turn around and glare at the blood-red characters.

Jiànzào

Construction.

Questions creep into my mind.

Don't get curious. What happens here doesn't concern you. It's not worth it. Go back to your job.

I bite my tongue.

My job. The cotton fields.

A blizzard trails down my spine.

You've got to go. Otherwise, there will be worse.

I sigh, rub my arms and haul my heavy body out of the hallway.

"That was *not* a minute," Mei exclaims when I'm close enough.

"I didn't mean literally," I respond.

"You were gone for *ten* minutes. I was about to have a heart attack. Please, don't do that again. I wasn't sure if...if you were going to come back."

I nod, the words clogged in my throat. "I'm sorry."

The rest of the time passes by in complete silence. I'm too ashamed to say anything. I shouldn't have left for this long.

This isn't the rest of the world. It's a place where one second can be the difference between life and death.

"COME HERE," the kind guard urges.

I drag myself to him and he reaches behind to grab his chains. "Your wrists?"

I hold my arms out and expect the cool, stiff metal surface to wrap around my wrists but they remain bare.

I look up into the guard's eyes. He's holding back tears and continues to stare at my wrists. I trace the direction of his eyes and glare at the raw, swollen flesh.

He drops the chains and holds himself loosely. I drop my arms, letting them swing beside me. The man sighs, holds a finger to his lips and opens the cell door. As it *creaks* shut, I smile and nod at him.

I lie down on the bare floor and let my bones

s

i

n

k

until I'm a boneless jellyfish. My mind drifts between dreams to reality as I close my eyes and let the darkness take me.

"STOP BEING unreasonable," a woman's voice tears through my dream.

My eyes flutter open and I crawl to the cell door. I stick my head out slightly to see a short, stern woman standing face-to-face with Chen. Her black hair flows a little past her shoulders and wisps of shorter hair fly in front of her face. Dark valleys lay under her eyes and her skin is slightly folded on her forehead. Her hand is curled in a fist beside her hip and the other is in the air.

The kind guard stands behind her, his face drained of all color. He stares down at his feet in shame and his fingers twirl behind his back.

"Give him a break," the woman basically yells at Chen.

"I decide this, not you," Chen replies, steel woven into his voice.

"No. I have a say in this and this is unreasonable. You're asking too much from Zhao."

"Huan, listen to me. *I* am your husband's boss so it is up to *me* to decide when he gets to leave work," Chen remarks patiently.

"He's been here for over three days. I don't even get to see him anymore. This is unfair, especially to your own brother."

Brother? Chen's brother? The guard is Chen's brother?

Huan grabs Zhao's hand and drags him along with her.

"We're leaving whether you like it or not. You are abusing Zhao."

Zhao stumbles behind her and Chen rubs the bridge of his nose.

"Fine, but he won't be paid as much."

"It doesn't matter," Huan calls out deep within a hallway. "What matters to me is my husband, not some paper."

Chen mutters to himself and sighs as if he's a disappointed father. He steps toward my cell and I dive into a corner, pretending to be asleep.

Crash.

I flinch, my heart pounding against my chest.

Crash.

I wrap my arms around myself, making sure I don't move. I crack my eyes open to see Chen punching a wall.

"Feng."

Silence.

"I guess I'll have to do this myself," Chen grumbles and disappears.

My breath escapes my throat and I take in the tense air. I close my eyes and try to think of happy things but Chen's punches still ring in my ear.

Thud. Thud.

Two distinct footsteps echo down the hall. I shut my eyes tight and retreat deeper into the shadows of the corner.

"Unfortunately, my *sister-in-law* decided to drag her husband back home. I don't have a guard to keep an eye on this prisoner. I'm willing to pay you extra if you don't mind taking over tonight," Chen grumbles.

"Sir, you don't have to pay me. This is my duty. I must protect my country from these *Zuìfàn*. I will gladly take the job forever, if you want," a mysterious, sly voice replies.

Chen chuckles. "Your enthusiasm is much appreciated. However, I need you to keep your current job downstairs. There isn't anyone more suitable than you for that job. This is just a one-night thing."

My heart hammers against my ribs and my blood goes cold.

This man is in charge of the

Black

Rooms.

5

BESH

CHEN'S FOOTSTEPS GROW muffled until they become hushed taps. The man, Feng, leans against the wall, his head bobbing slightly and his eyes drooping down.

Until suddenly, he swings his head in my direction.

I shut my eyes and clench my hands, trying to erase his hungry eyes from my mind.

Thud. Thud.

My ears perk up as he silently makes his way toward the cell door.

Cling.

He grips the bars.

THUMPTHUMP. THUMPTHUMP.

My breathing becomes shallow and my eyes beg to open.

"Hmmm," Feng grunts.

I jump up and press against the wall, glaring at the man shaking the cell door.

"Come here, *little girl,"* he says slyly.

I stay where I am.

I can't move.

I can't breathe.

I can't speak.

I'm frozen in place.

"I know you're awake. I can see you." He pauses. "If you don't come here, I'll go there."

Cling. Cling.

The jingling of keys near the door makes my heart pound.

You have to go to him before he comes to you.

I heft myself off the ground and make my way to the door.

"I'm not as nice as Zhao, you know. Where are your restraints?"

The words clump in my throat and a few slurred sounds come out of my mouth.

"It seems Zhao has a soft spot, hm?"

"N—No, sir," I sputter.

"No?" He asks, a smirk growing on his face.

"I took them off, sir," I say, bracing myself.

"You took them off?" he says, emphasizing each letter.

"Yes, sir."

"Now, the question is, how did a *child* manage to get metal handcuffs off? Even a grown man can't." Feng analyzes me suspiciously.

"They were a little loose, sir. I was able to get them off."

"Loose? That sounds like Zhao didn't do a good job."

I mentally slap myself. I should have thought about this more. Now, Zhao is going to get in trouble.

Feng's grin widens. "Well, someone is going to have to put those back on. Bring them over to me."

I grab the chains and hand them to him. Without saying a word, he grabs my wrists through the bars and fastens them together. He tugs down and attaches my wrists to my ankles.

"All done," Feng articulates and he crosses his arms, entertained.

I roll over to the corner and close my eyes. My mind begins to wander and—

"Stand up! Those who are unwilling to become slaves!

Take our flesh, and build it to become a new Great Wall!

The Chinese people have reached a most dangerous time."

Feng's voice gets louder and louder with each word and the letters *bang* on my head like a drum. Soon, his singing is accompanied by drumming.

He's not going to let me sleep.

Through the wall, I hear Mama stir and groan.

Don't wake up. Please don't wake up, Mama.

A whimper echoes through my cell, the tears from the other side ringing in my ears.

Please stop crying, Mama. Please.

But she doesn't.

I want to throw Feng off the building for waking her up.

Her tears slowly dry up and so does my mind, even with the singing and drumming.

"TIME FOR WORK," Zhao calls out.

But I've barely slept for two hours.

My eyes weigh down and my mind is numb. Feng's off-note singing still rings in my ears. I collapse back onto the floor.

Creeeeaaak.

"Come on, you have to get up, *Háizi.* Chen will be here soon," Zhao shakes me.

I sit up, my eyes still closed, and grip my head. My brain moves in my head from Zhao's force.

He walks out of the cell and gestures for me to come out. I trudge out into the hallway and glance back.

He looks at me, nods and smiles.

"Attention. Everyone report to the facility's entrance," a robotic, female voice resonates.

Everyone drops their sacks and darts away. A hand grips my wrist and I let Mei drag me to the assembly. On the raised platform, Chen and Ürkesh stand with

Bao.

Bao is here.

My mind freezes.

"*Qiúfàn*, please join me in welcoming my dear friend, Bao. He is one of the best supervisors out there. Coming from me, this is an honor, right Bao?"

"Welcome, o mighty Bao," a dull chorus booms.

Bao smiles and nods. "Thank you, o honorable Chen. I'm honored to be visiting your prestigious camp. Chen is someone to look up to. A role model, some may say." Bao scans the crowd and when he spots me, his smile fades.

I squirm internally and shift my feet.

Please stop looking at me. Please stop looking at me.

"I hope you all don't get too *comfortable* in this facility. You wouldn't want to go back to mine, would you?" He grits his teeth as the words spit out of his mouth.

I can feel his eyes drilling through my skull.

"I hope you all will give Bao a warm welcome and show him how much better this camp is compared to his."

Bao's eyes catch on fire when he hears Chen's remarks. Chen playfully slaps Bao on the back.

"It's just a joke, my friend. Some friendly competition," Chen laughs with Bao but the sparks remain in his eyes.

"Everyone is dismissed. I expect double the work to be done due to this break."

The wave of people parts in different directions, as if they're multiple rivers. I make it a few steps into the crowd before a hand rests on my shoulder. I'm pulled and twisted backward, staring straight into the eyes of my former supervisor,

Bao.

6

ALTE

"YOU'RE SUPPOSED TO BE DEAD," Bao states, scanning me. "I killed you with my bare hands."

I swallow my shock. "I...I don't know what you are talking about, sir."

"Master. Call me master."

"I'm sorry...m...master. I didn't know," I stammer.

"You didn't know? You're the girl from my camp. The pesky one."

"I...I don't know what you are talking about."

His face hardens. "I had a girl who looked *exactly* like you in my camp a few weeks ago." He searches deeply into my eyes. "But she had a particular fire in her eyes. She was rebellious, fiery. I don't see that in you. It's like you're a broken version of her."

Don't let him get to you. Don't let him get to you.

"Chen! Come here," Bao calls out from over his shoulder.

When Chen arrives, he looks to me and then Bao. The corners of his lips raise. "I see you've met my stepdaughter."

I cringe.

"Your stepdaughter? You have children with a Uyghur woman?" Bao explodes.

"I *was* married to a Uyghur woman back when I was a naive boy. She is my ex-wife's daughter from another marriage. Kai. Come here. Bao, meet my son, Kai. Kai, this is Bao."

My eyes bulge out of their sockets.

"*That* is your son?" Bao yells.

"Yes. Is there a problem?" Chen asks.

"Bu...He...Camp...Wha..."

"I know. I know. He looks just like me. You leave," Chen tells Ürkesh.

"No...he...was in my camp. He was the one who made it all the way to Pakistan and then disappeared off the radar."

"That's the thing. He didn't disappear off the radar. I caught him and," Chen leans into Bao's ear, "I brainwashed him. He doesn't remember anything except what I've told him."

The air rushes out of my lungs. *Brainwashed him? Chen brainwashed Ürkesh? No wonder he has been acting distant. He doesn't know who I am. He doesn't know who he is.*

A blur of movement snaps me out of my trance. From the corner of my eye, Mei hides behind a shed and watches me.

I move one hand behind my back and motion for her to go back but she doesn't. She remains where she is, still as a statue.

I give up and resume watching Bao and Chen. Bao's face is still bleached and his eyes are smaller while Chen is going on and on about how he's transformed Ürkesh.

"What about her, your stepdaughter?" Bao asks. Both of their eyes turn toward me. "Wasn't she in my camp?"

"Yes. You don't remember?" Chen asks, puzzled.

"But she's supposed to be dead," Bao exclaims.

"Well, she clearly isn't but she will be if she doesn't follow orders, isn't that right?"

I nod, swallowing the brick in my throat.

"I have to get back to work now but if you have any more questions, feel free to ask." Chen walks away, leaving me and Bao behind. Bao clenches his jaw and tightens his fist.

"You'll be dead soon enough, *Zuìfàn,*" he says and storms off.

A shadow creeps close.

"Come on," Mei murmurs and I free my feet from the roots holding them down.

Once the little white clouds come into sight, I take in the heavy air. "What was that all about?" Mei asks.

"Bao was suspicious."

"Suspicious about what?"

"It's nothing, really."

"Why do you look shaken up then?"

"It's really nothing. Don't worry about it," I repeat.

Her face hardens slightly as her mouth curls into a frown. "If you say so," she mutters and focuses on her work.

The sky is pitch-black, the stars and moon hiding behind the thick clouds. The birds have withdrawn to their warm homes. The crickets have become still and silent and the slumber of the world outside keeps me wide awake.

An image of a family of birds floats into my head. The loving parents and feisty children sleeping together. Nothing can separate them.

But we get less than them. We are treated worse than animals. Worse than anything that exists.

Thud. Thud.

Heavy footsteps storm closer and closer and I sit up in the shadowed corner. The towering figure of my brother comes into sight and stops just before my cell. He peers around and his face clouds.

"Where is Zhao," he mutters under his breath. "Zhao. Zhao. *Zhao.*"

A door shuts somewhere and a panting Zhao darts into the light.

"Oh, Kai. I thought you were Chen."

"Father sent me to check on you because he had a feeling you weren't doing your job properly. He was right."

"I was quickly checking on something but otherwise, I haven't left my position. Give your uncle a break. I have a life outside of this building as well."

"Fine but next time, I *will* tell Father." His face softens when he sees Zhao yawning. "I can take over your shift for today. You can go home and sleep."

"What?" Zhao exclaims.

"I can take over your shift for today, if you want," Ürkesh repeats.

"Are you sure?" Zhao asks, confusion plastered on his face.

"Yes. You are my uncle, after all, and you deserve a break," Ürkesh beams and I secretly smile with him.

"Re...really? Thanks."

He nods to Ürkesh and leaves. The instant Zhao's footsteps disappear, I jump up and fly to the cell door.

"Ürkesh?" I peep.

"How many times do I have to tell you that my name is not Ürkesh? My name is Kai. Kai. Kai." His eyes light on fire and smoke flies out of his ears.

I nod and glance down toward my feet for a few seconds before meeting his eyes. I steel my jaw.

"Kai, I know what he did to you."

"Who?"

"Chen."

"*My* father? You know what *my* father did?"

"Yes. He brainwa—"

"You think you know *so* much. Well, guess what? You Uyghurs are all *liars*." He scoffs.

I get louder. *"He* did this to you."

"What '*this*?' He saved my life. But you wouldn't know that. You don't know anything."

We begin speaking over each other but his words go in one ear and out the other. The only thing I can hear is me.

My voice.

My words.

My desperation.

"He's the reason you're different. He took you away from us, from *me*. He made you forget who I am. Who you are. Who everyone is. He's infected your mind with lies about everything: your family, your people. He—"

"Shut up! Shutupshutupshutup."

He holds onto the bars and glares into my eyes.

His fury,

His fire,

His hate,

All of it is Chen's.

Chen has made Ürkesh his clone.

And I can't bring him back.

He pants like a bull. "If you say anything like that about my father again, I will tear you to pieces. *Do you understand?*"

He shakes the bars hard and I jerk backward. Ürkesh calms down and sits down in a chair. I crawl back to my pitch-black corner and hug my knees.

My blood boils.

My heart hammers, screaming,

Come back.

Come back.

Come back.

But he doesn't.

Ürkesh doesn't come back.

My brother doesn't come back.

He's gone

Silent tears flood out of my eyes and I swallow the whimpers clogged in my chest. I bury my face into my legs.

I wish I could leave.

I wish I could go back.

I wish I could be at home, where everything was normal.

I wish none of this happened.

I wish this was all a dream.

I wish.

I wish.

I wish.

Black floods in, wrapping around me. A warmth settles down as the tears begin to slow down. My mind shuts down and I collapse as the wind outside whispers,

Shhhhhhhh.

GENTLE, SLOW MURMURS drift me out of my sleep. I sit up and shake my head but it continues. I press my ear against the wall.

"So truly with hardship comes ease, truly with hardship comes ease."

My eyes widen and my mouth drops, hanging on my chin.

She's reciting the Quran.

At that moment, distant footsteps grow crisper with each passing second.

The woman scrambles and the sound of paper crunching resonates through the wall.

"You're a minute late. Chen has ordered that you will be allowed back in your cells an hour after everyone else," Zhao announces and shakes his head secretly.

Click. Click.

He opens my cell door and another one.

He only used to open mine.

Out from the cell emerges a middle-aged woman with sharp, short hair. A few strands of silver sparkle among the black. Her lips are cracked, like her eyes. She glances toward me for a moment and then forces her eyes down.

She knows.

She knows that I know.

She knows that I heard.

Zhao looks at the both of us. "Please, follow me. Chen wants to observe you today. He wants to check whether you are fit to be around everyone else." He swallows hard.

We follow him to a different wing of the camp, Zhao in the front and me in the back. The hall is like a black hole compared to what I'm used to, with only a few lights along the way. The cell doors lay wide open, with chains being the only object in the cells. Closed doors with letters and numbers written on them fly by every few seconds.

A326

B031

C529

Until we reach an open door.

The room is bright white. There's almost nothing in there, except for a large screen on the wall. Chen is in the center of the room, pacing back and forth like the pendulum in an ancient clock.

For the first time, I focus on his face. He resembles Ürkesh but not much. Wrinkles are scratched on his face and dark circles shadow his eyes. The only thing that is really similar between the two are their expressions.

That's when a thought surfaces in my mind.

He's a human...just like us.

A pang of sympathy bursts through me.

It's the government's fault, not his. The government corrupted him and fed him lies about us.

But at the same time, my heart squirms.

He should have the conscience to know what's right and wrong. He should know what he's doing is wrong. He should treat us for who we are rather than dirt. He has a part in this too.

The blue and red crash inside me until the red ultimately wins.

It doesn't matter whether he's stressed or tired. He is a grown man who can reason. His conscience should be telling him that he is hurting other people.

"You called for them," Zhao breaks the silence.

"Yes. You may leave now," Chen says as he exhales loudly. Zhao bows and walks out of the room, leaving the two of us.

Alone.

With Chen.

I swallow my fear and stare down at my feet. The woman next to me does the same.

She's new. She doesn't know how it works here.

Chen stops his pacing and faces us. "Do you two know why you are here?" he asks.

"No, sir."

"Of course you don't. You both have a record of *misbehaving*, especially you." He points at me. "However, I am merciful, not cruel. Therefore, I've decided to give you both a chance, *one* chance, to be let out of isolation. If you fail, you will be kept in your current cell, separated forever. Understand?"

We nod.

"Good. Look here."

Our eyes flicker to the projection of China's president,

The leader of this genocide.

Xi Jinping.

"Who is this man?"

Silence.

"*Tsk, tsk,* neither of you will pass the test *if you don't answer.* What is this man's name?"

One of us has to say something.

"Xi Jinping," I respond.

"At least one of you isn't mute. Who is Xi Jinping?"

"Our president," the woman answers.

"And..." Chen pauses, waiting for an answer.

"Our...our savior," I whisper.

"What has he saved you from?"

I whiz back to Bao's camp and the dull murmur of the man reading the textbook rings in my ear.

"He has saved us from our natural rebellious tendencies. He has 're-educated' us into being civilized and human again."

"This would be an excellent answer if I was foolish. You're reading off a textbook. Do you believe what you just said?"

I keep myself from hesitating. "Yes, sir."

"Do you believe it with your whole heart?"

My back stiffens. "Yes, sir," I respond.

"What about you?" Chen turns to the woman next to me. She doesn't say anything.

She'll get herself killed.

I turn slightly and tap her elbow lightly with mine.

Crack.

I grip my throbbing cheek. Chen lowers himself to meet my eyes. "She can speak for herself, *Gǒu.*"

I inch back to my original spot and the woman's eyes flutter toward me. I move my head by a few millimeters, encouraging her to answer.

"Yes, sir. I believe it," she says, her voice heavy and glum.

"Hmm." Chen snatches a remote from the table.

Click.

The image of Xi Jinping disappears and is replaced by an image of a Uyghur and a Han man standing side by side.

"Who are these two?"

This time, the woman responds. "A Uyghur and a Han man standing next to each other."

"Can you tell the difference between the two?"

"The Uyghur has a beard and…"

"And," Chen nudges.

"They look nothing alike," the woman turns the other way, her eyes steely.

"Yes, that is correct. Tell me, which one is the better of the two?" Chen asks me.

"The second," I respond.

"What ethnicity is the *second* part of?"

I close my eyes. "He is Han Chinese."

"So…"

"He is better than the Uyghur man," I spit.

Click.

This time, the pictures move. I swallow my gasp. A guard pounds a man with his baton, spitting curses. The Uyghur man's face is stained with tears and blood. He begs the guard, screaming and crying.

The video freezes.

"Let me give you some context. This man,"—he points at the bloody heap—"stole bread but was caught. He proceeded to give excuses: 'my family is poor,' 'we don't have enough money,' 'my children are starving.' You *Yěmán rén* think you can lie to a soldier? We are not as gullible as you think. The noble guard punished this felon for his crime. Now, tell me, what is the Uyghur man's mistake?"

My heart sinks into my stomach.

"Hmm? What's the Uyghur's mistake?"

"He stole from the Han and lied to them about it," I croak.

"Good. Both of you are doing well in this test. Maybe, just maybe you might become civilized one day."

Click.

He turns the projector off. "Now, onto the final part of your test. What do you both think about your religion?"

I can't lie about this.

I can't

I can't

I can't.

I swallow the brick in my throat but none of the words come out of my mouth.

"Are you both mute now?" Chen taunts.

We both remain silent. He walks to the woman.

"Do you believe in Allah?" he booms.

She raises her chin up to meet his fiery eyes. "Yes, I do," she responds, not a hint of fear woven in her voice.

The air grows heavy.

Crack.

Chen backhands the woman and she jerks backward.

"That's a fraction of what you will get,"—he turns to me—"You should have learned your lesson from her. Do. You. Believe. In. Allah?"

My heart slows down and I straighten myself to meet Chen's eyes.

"I do," I croak, expecting a lightning bolt from the sky to strike down on me.

I blink.

Smoke climbs out of Chen's ears but he remains glued to the floor.

"Zhao. Guards. *Come in here this instant.*"

Thud.

Thud.

THUD.

THUDTHUD.

I take in a deep breath and brace myself.

"These two have completely *failed* the test." Zhao's sad eyes meet mine and he shakes his head.

"Keep them separated from everyone else. No mercy for either of them. I'm done with this. *I'm done with them.*"

The other guards grip the woman's arms and lead her away roughly while Zhao gently nudges me to follow him.

I comply, but not before glaring at Chen.

"You're going to stay in here for a few days. Chen wants you to think about your actions," Zhao leans in to whisper, "Please listen to him. I can't see him hurt anyone anymore. Please."

I don't answer.

Because I can't.

I can't lie about myself.

I can't lie about my beliefs.

I can't lie about Allah.

"Promise me," he begs.

"I can't."

"Please, *Háizi*. Please."

"I'm sorry, but I can't. I can't lie about that."

He surrenders back to his station, his mouth glued in an upside-down 'U.' His defeat burns a hole through my heart. I can't make a promise I'll break.

Hmmmhh. Hmmmmh.

Gentle muttering perks my ears up and I make my way back to the wall. I press my ear against the cold stone wall and relax, taking in every word.

"What's this?" Chen bursts.

I jerk back from the wall.

"You. Are. Writing. This? This illegal material? Where did you get the paper? Who gave it to you? Zhao? Did you?"

Click.

Chen's voice gets closer.

"How *dare* you? How *dare* you disobey me and the government? I'm going to make you an example for everyone here. *Don't you worry.* First, you disobey me in words, and now actions? You think you'll get away with this?"

Within a few seconds, there is complete silence on the other side of the wall. I press my ear against the wall, listening for any sign of life.

Heavy footsteps interrupt my thoughts and I jerk back into my cell. Ürkesh emerges from the shadows.

Click.

He unlocks the cell door. "Father is calling all prisoners to assemble."

I nod and follow him. My mind wanders emptily until I reach a familiar door.

The door that led to the construction area.

I enter the once-forbidden area as a wave of people flood in. I'm swept to the front and freeze in place.

It's a new torture chamber.

My heart climbs into my throat.

I glance at the people beside me and follow their gaze upward.

Chen.

Chen holds the woman on a platform above a massive, water-filled glass tank. The water below reaches up, slapping the nooses hanging a few inches above.

It's the perfect punishment.

Bam. Bam.

The doors shut behind us, locking us all in.

"Everyone, let me introduce you to prisoner A3891. She has committed many, many serious crimes. She stole paper and a pencil to write illegal material.

"This *Gǒu* is a threat to the safety of China. It is in our great fortune that I caught her before she could cause any more trouble. And yet, she still doesn't admit her crimes. What a *Yě shòu*.

"Those who disobey the Han are always punished. Those *Uyghurs* who think they can fool us are always punished. This woman must then be punished, don't you think?"

Silence.

"Should she be punished?" Chen roars.

"Everything you do is correct," everyone replies, only their mouths moving.

I remain still.

He reaches forward and grabs a noose.

"If any one of you takes your eyes off her, you'll *never, ever* see the light of day again," Chen booms.

He wraps the noose around the woman's neck, tightening it. Her eyes widen for a split second but she covers up the shock, her face lighting on fire.

He takes a step back and the woman turns slightly. A muscle in Chen's neck twitches.

"This is going to be fun," he mutters, a hungry grin spreading across his face.

Chen darts toward the woman as her mouth drops. His shoulder slams into her back and the pulley holding the noose zips forward.

Plonk.

The woman is dunked into the water, the noose digging into her neck. White bubbles become a growing storm around her. She claws at the rope around her neck, her legs kicking and back thrashing. The white around her wraps around its victim.

Until she becomes still.

A still,

lifeless,

hanging body.

My eyes burn.

My lungs gulp for air.

My heart screams.

All around me, a sea of eyes turns in my direction. The hollow, widened eyes lock with mine as a pair of sharp, red ones creep

closer

and

closer,

Until the sea parts and the towering man glares down at me.

A boulder lodges in my throat as the last bubble of air raises up in the water.

7

YETTE

CHEN'S EYES TURN WILD. *"I warned all of you that I would not be merciful,"* he booms.

"But I didn't do anything wrong."

"You did. You *flinched*. You disobeyed my instructions, just like she did. You deserve to be *executed* but," a hungry grin spreads across his face, "I'll take my time."

"I didn't. I didn't do anything wrong," I plead.

"They'll be the judge of that," he turns to everyone else, "Did. She. Flinch?"

Everyone turns into stone, their eyes wide. After a minute of hesitating, they nod.

My heart

S　H　A　T　T　E　R　S

Chen grabs my arm and I'm pulled out of the crowd.

My heart hammers. The words are stuck in my throat.

Help.

Help.

Help.

"Please, sir. *Please*. I didn't mean it. I really didn't. *Please have mercy*," I beg.

"I've been too lenient with you. You've been taking advantage of my kindness. You need to be punished before you go too far."

"It won't happen again. I promise, sir. *Please*," I shriek but it's too late.

I stumble on the ground and pass cells overflowing with people.

"Please. Help. Help."

But they all remain frozen in place.

But Chen doesn't stop.

I pass by Mama's cell.

"Mama. Mama. Help me. Help me."

Mama turns to look at me and her eyes widen. Her eyes flood and she crumbles onto the floor, sobbing.

But Chen doesn't stop.

Because he doesn't care.

He doesn't care about my screams.

My pleas.

My tears.

Nothing.

I struggle in his grip but his hand is like a chain linked to my wrist. I'm nothing compared to it.

Nothing

At

All

"Let. Me. Go." I claw at his fingers as I continue stumbling,

And stumbling,

And stumbling on the floor.

Click. Creeeeeak.

The door screams open and I'm flung into it. A wave of arms crashes down onto me as the faint light becomes black. Ropes and chains wrap around me like snakes.

A rough surface appears underneath me and the wave of guards retreats.

I'm tied to a chair.

I pull at my wrists but the ropes bite deeper into my skin. Shadows emerge from the corners of my eyes. From the walls, towering soldiers wearing black circle around me.

These aren't the same soldiers that I've seen. They're bigger, stronger.

My heart collapses.

They're wearing masks. The only part of their body that's visible are their eyes. Ice travels through my veins.

One of them reaches behind their back and a long, metal rod comes out. The rest do the same. They hold their sticks in a defensive position, circling their prey.

"Have fun, boys," Chen chuckles as he closes the door.

Thwack.

Thwack.

Crack.

MY EYES peel open and my head weighs down on the stone floor. I try to lift myself up but a flash of white pain shoots up my body. My clothes cling to my skin. I peer down to see a pool of crimson spreading around me.

A hot breath rushes out of my lungs as I try to inhale.

Kkkaaa. Kkkaaa.

I cough as the tense, metallic air surges through my body. The room smells like...blood.

I painfully sit up, grasp the chair and hoist myself off the ground. My knees collapse as I crumple back onto the floor.

It's as if I don't have any bones.

My vision clears up and the room laughs at me. Streaks of red paint the black wall and the wooden chair. I tear my hand off it with terror.

I need to get out.

I pull myself against the floor, inching closer to the door. My legs wobble as I lift myself up.

Krrn. Krrn.

The knob doesn't budge. Bile rises in my throat and the smell gets stronger. Reality washes over me.

This really isn't a dream.

This is real.

The room is real.

The blood is real.

I *am real.*

Tears well up in my eyes and this time, I can't stop them. One drips down my cheek, its *splat* echoing in the barren room.

Knock. Knock.

Heavy rapping vibrates the door. My tears retreat back into their hideout and I crawl away from the door. It shrieks open.

Zhao steps into the room.

I bite my tongue.

"Let's get you out of here," he whispers.

I stand up but collapse back onto the floor. My legs can't support my weight. He sighs gently, helps me up and we slowly walk back to my cell.

I LAY AGAINST the cold stone floor. My back stings and my limbs ache but I stay still. Footsteps come in and out of the hallway and as the *thuds* get louder, my nerves tingle. The sky outside is tinted with pink and orange but I've only slept for a few hours.

Rushed footsteps creep closer and closer until the deafening sound pierces my ears. I turn my head toward the door and see Ürkesh staring straight at me.

There's something different about him. His eyes are...softer. The usual fire isn't eating at them.

"Time to get to work," he commands.

I try to pick myself off the floor but I can't. I slam back onto the ground. Zhao puts his hand on Ürkesh's shoulder.

"Leave her be," he says.

Ürkesh sighs. "Father said that she has to work today. He can't afford to have a worker down for another day."

"She can't move. We don't even know if she's broken something. Her body is bruised. Ask your father if she can have another day off."

Ürkesh nods and my heart leaps.

Maybe he's closer to being back. Maybe he's closer to remembering.

But my hopeless heart whispers something else.

He doesn't remember who you are. He never will. He's not closer to being your brother again.

Thud. Thud.

These footsteps sound different. They aren't Ürkesh's and they aren't Zhao's.

"Zhao," the voice calls out and my heart stops beating.

It's Chen.

I scramble to press myself further into the corner. *"Zhao.* Come here."

"Coming, sir," Zhao responds from the other side of the hallway.

A few seconds later, Zhao darts into the light. "What is *wrong* with you? We can't have a prisoner take a break for a day. That means at least five bags of cotton."

"*Dìdì*, listen to me. She is injured. An injured worker is an unproductive one. If she goes into the fields, she could die. A dead prisoner does not benefit you in any way, shape or form. You would lose five bags a dayPlease, give her a few days to recover."

"*A few days?* I don't have that kind of time. Why am I even asking you? I'm the one in charge here, not you."

"I shouldn't have to remind you that the reason she isn't able to work is because *you* punished her. She wouldn't be in this state if it wasn't for you."

"Don't raise your voice at me."

They break out into a verbal fight.

"I'm *your* older brother. You shouldn't raise *your* voice at *me*," Zhao screams.

"I'm the one who doesn't act childish," Chen responds.

"It's not *my* fault that our parents valued strength over intellect. It's not my fault they were never satisfied with what I accomplished. It's not my fault I was never good enough."

"You're just jealous that I'm better than you—"

"You are *not* better than me," Zhao interrupts.

"The reason I'm *better* than you is because you let your kindness hold you back. You have to help everyone that comes across your path, don't you?"

Zhao's face drops and the tense silence settles into the building.

Click.

"Get up, *Xíngshi*," Chen commands.

He grips my wrist and pulls me up. "You've had enough time to rest. You wouldn't be in this state if you would have followed directions. If you don't want to be punished, you'd better fill six sacks of cotton—to the top."

"Yes, sir," I croak, my ribs stinging. I limp out of the cell. Zhao's head is hung down. He doesn't meet my eyes as I drag myself outside.

"What. Happened?" Mei blurts after I painfully crawl to her.

I don't say anything. I don't need to say anything. She knows.

Mei helps me lie down on the dirt. "I'll fill your share. Just rest and recover. You probably have a broken something. You can't work"

"No, I'll do it. You don't need to do two people's work."

I struggle to get up but she nudges me back down. "If I see Chen coming, we'll get you up and he'll never know. You can't keep going like this. You have to trust. You have to trust *me*. I'm here to hold your hand so we can survive this *together*. That can't happen if you don't accept my hand."

I nod because I know she's right, no matter how much I want her to be wrong. I have to trust.

I take a deep breath and lie back down. Mei opens both sacks and rips the cotton off their stalks, filling the brown bags with clouds.

Guilt nibbles at my heart.

She shouldn't have to do my work. I need to fend for myself. I can't drag her down with me. It's not fair that she does double the work while I rest in the dirt.

A sharp pain in my side makes me remember why I'm resting.

If you don't rest, you won't be able to recover, which means you'll have more trouble working. Chen will punish you more and your pain will just get worse.

I turn my head to watch Mei work. She's immersed, her mind fully encompassed by cotton. Beads of sweat drip down her face and her fingers are coated in brown sap.

She's so young. It isn't fair to her, to us. We shouldn't have to sacrifice our lives for the Chinese government. They're just trying to gain profit while killing us. That's all they care about. Money, not people.

"Stop worrying, Hala. Relax and enjoy, even if it is difficult. You need to recover mentally too, not just physically."

I smile at her. "Okay."

I watch as the clouds soar through the sky. They become shapes and then people, enacting a story.

My story.

The soldiers taking everything away.

Bao's camp.

Uncle Shan.

Escaping the country.

Mama.

Being forced back here.

Ürkesh.

As the hours fly by, strings of orange and pink weave into the blue sky. The sun glows red and retreats to sleep as the workers slowly trickle back into the cells.

Mei grunts as she heaves the last bag of cotton onto her shoulders. "Let's go. We don't want to be late."

She helps me up and my back pops. One day of rest has made me feel more relaxed. It's been a long time since I've done absolutely nothing.

"Thanks," I say.

"For what?"

"For everything." I point at the bag.

"It's nothing, really. We've got to be there for each other if we want to live. None of us can survive on our own."

The scene of the woman drowning replays in my head. Beads of sweat drip down my face and my heart races.

You could be next. You need to get out.

We walk back to the prison in silence. "Mei...I was thinking..."

"Yes?"

"Never mind, it's dangerous."

"We'll never know if it's actually dangerous if you don't tell me," she peeps.

"Well, we've...I've never thought about escaping until now. It doesn't seem *impossible.*"

"What about your brother?" she asks.

I swallow hard. "I don't think he's my brother anymore. I can't wait because I assume he's going to come back. The best chance is to escape and tell someone. Maybe they'll be able to do something. Maybe they'll make him come back. We...need to at least try."

You know that's not true. Everyone knows but they're not doing anything.

"And your mother?" she asks.

"We can try to take her with us?"

Mei stares into empty space for a few seconds. Her face is pale as if she's just seen someone die.

"I...I don't know."

"I understand if you don't want to come with me but I'm going no matter what."

"But...I can't let you go alone."

My heart flutters.

"I don't really have anything to lose," she sighs, "I'll go with you."

I nod and smile at her. "We'll need to prepare and find a safe way out so we can avoid the security cameras."

"I know a way," Mei peeps, a gentle smile spreading across her face.

The excitement of leaving blows the sleep out of me. I glance up at the bland ceiling, dreaming about escaping the country.

We need to go somewhere farther than Kazakhstan. It's too close to China's power. We can't be taken again.

A warm rain washes down on me.

The skeptic in me emerges. '*You don't know that this plan will be successful. There is a very, very low chance of you actually escaping China and an even lower chance of you getting far enough. On the other hand, there is a very high chance that you or Mei will be killed once Chen does catch you.*'

You don't know that.

'I do. You know I'm right. Ürkesh tried escaping over three times and look at him now. He doesn't remember who he really is.'

That's a different case.

'How is it different?'

I have to try though. My...Our lives depend on it. Maybe other people can help us.

'You're in an illusion. The facts are right in front of you. No one is coming for you or anyone else. It's just a matter of survival now.'

Just stop. Let me be hopeful. Hope all I have left. That 'very, very low' chance could become a reality. I just need to try.

The voice doesn't come back but the doubts it has sown have been planted in my heart.

8

SEKKIZ

"IS THIS A good spot to bury this?" Mei asks, pointing to a patch of loose soil.

"I think. None of the guards would search here and they're definitely not going to start digging."

She nods. "Now, rest. You need it. You won't be able to run properly if you're injured."

"But—"

"No 'buts.' You have to rest *now*. I'll deal with your share."

I want to argue but her eyes are filled with steely resolve. She's not going to let me argue.

I lay down without peeping another sound. You can't argue with a wall. I close my eyes and memories flood my mind.

Memories of what my life used to be.

My whole life flies in front of my eyes.

The ghosts of people who used to be there *whoosh* by me.

I drift between reality and dreams. Slowly, the darkness comes in, wrapping its icy blanket around me.

"Hala. Hala. *Hala,*" Mama shrieks, the bloodcurdling screams piercing my ears.

"I'm here, Mama. I'm here," I call out but no one responds.

"*Hala. Hala.*" Mama's voice grows more and more panicked and my heart begins to pound faster and faster. I try to move forward but I fall to the ground. I look down to find my feet

S   I

N

K

I

N

G

into the ground.

I grip the dirt, trying to pull myself out but I just sink deeper.

"Hala. Hala."

"I'm coming, Mama. I'm coming," I scream.

I try to climb out but now, the dirt is at my waist. Desperation strikes my heart as my stomach sinks. The dirt climbs higher until only my head is out. I shut my eyes and

I stop sinking.

I open my eyes to find red pupils staring back at me. I try to squirm but I'm frozen in the dirt.

"Now you can't struggle, can you?" Chen cackles.

"No, she can't, my dear friend," Bao appears from the shadows.

Both of them are dressed in complete black and in their hands are metal rods.

My eyes widen and I swallow a scream.

Crack.

A bolt of lightning strikes me from the sky. My head snaps to the side.

"You're not getting away this time." Chen and Bao have now combined and both of their faces pop out of a single body.

Crack.

Crack.

CRACK.

CRACK.

I gulp in air as I shoot up. Beads of glistening sweat drips down my face and I reach for my neck.

"Are you okay?" Mei asks.

"Yeah. I'm fine," I wheeze.

It was just a dream.

I touch my face, just to make sure it's in place. I can still feel the cool rods cracking my bones.

I sit like that for a while, trying to get my breathing regulated but the air remains tense and heavy.

Mei looks back at me frequently but she doesn't say anything. I hold my breath and my heart finally slows down. I fall back onto the dirt.

Stop being ridiculous. The ground can't swallow you. It was just a nightmare that will never happen.

"But it was so real," I whisper back to myself.

A brick lodges in my throat and scratches its way down. An uneasy feeling settles in my stomach.

I glare at the clouds, waiting for the sun to retreat but the minutes pass by like hours. The agonizing anticipation bites at my heart.

When?

When?

When?

After what feels like days, Mei grunts and lifts the bag.

"Is that the last one?" I ask.

She nods and I sit up.

"We can't leave right now. We have to wait for everything to settle down. We can't risk getting caught."

"Okay," I sigh and continue waiting.

"HALA. HALA. Get up."

I stir awake and sit up, Mei's figure clearing up.

"What?" I ask.

She sighs. "We have to escape tonight, remember?"

"One more minute."

She shakes me awake. "No. We have to leave *now*. The guards will come back in a few minutes. This is the only window of time we have."

My brain finally activates and my eyes pull open. "Let's go...Wait...what are you doing in my cell?"

She flashes the metallic object and we step into the faint light of the hallway. We turn toward Mama's cell. I peer in to see a withered figure on the ground.

"Mama?" I whisper.

The figure stirs slightly.

"Mama?"

She sits up, the white of her eyes shining in the dark. "Ha...Hala?"

I hold my hand out through the cell bars. Mama pulls her knees close.

"What are you doing?" she asks, loudly. I sink into the ground and glance behind my shoulder.

"Shh. Mama, please. Come on."

"No. *No.* We'll get caught. They'll kill us." Her voice gets louder and louder with each word. My heart pounds in my ears.

Click. Click. Click.

"Halt."

Mei's arms shoot straight up into the air and a swarm of pistols stares at our faces.

No

      No

            No

"Did you *seriously* expect to leave undetected?" The swarm parts for Chen and he points at the ceiling. "There are security cameras everywhere. There is always someone watching. But to have the *audacity* to think you could make it? No wonder you prisoners are all *Mógui.*"

Chen pauses and looks at his brother.

"And I have my older brother to thank," Zhao's eyes shift down as his brother's smirk grows, "He informed me of this plan after he noticed you on the camera. He's finally done something right for once. Something important, something significant, something good enough"

Chen chuckles as Zhao glances at us in shame.

I'm sorry, he mouths but it's not enough to heal the hurt,

To cool the anger,

To reverse the betrayal.

My heart squirms inside as my body turns numb. It's as if I'm up in the ceiling, watching myself surrounded by the soldiers and Chen.

It seems...unreal.

Chen lets the silence sink in. "This is the last straw. Both of you have made mistakes before and I've been merciful. You were just *children* after all but now, I'm done being kind. You both will pay, especially *you*," he points at me, "I warned you that if you make me angry, you will bear the consequences. Last time, I just punished you. This time, there is someone else who will pay as well."

His eyes dart toward Mama's cell and my heart shatters like glass. My blood freezes and the world begins to sway.

Back

        and forth.

Back

        and forth.

Back

        and forth

My stomach bubbles, fizzes and sinks deeper. I open my mouth to speak but only inaudible sounds come out.

I can't move.

I can't speak.

I can't breathe.

"First," his eyes turn toward Mei, "I have to deal with you. You've been in this camp for too long. You need a *new environment.*"

Mei's eyes widen and beg but she doesn't say anything. The guards inch closer and wrap their claws around her

And drag her

away.

She doesn't resist.

She doesn't beg.

She doesn't cry.

She doesn't know that I'm screaming inside.

That I'm crying, begging for her to come back.

Begging for her to not leave me alone.

But no one can hear the heart's tears.

Water floods into my eyes and I struggle to force it back down. I lift my eyes to look at Zhao. He's still staring at the ground, his eyes red and flooded with tears. He tries to hide them but it doesn't work. When Chen looks toward him, he turns away.

"I need to go home, *Dìdì,*" Zhao croaks.

"I didn't give you permission to leave. The best part is yet to come," Chen commands.

"Huan is waiting for me."

"What is she going to do if you arrive a little late? You have to stay so you can see how to control these *Núlì.* You're too soft on them."

Zhao opens his mouth to speak but Chen interrupts him. "I'm *not* taking no for an answer."

Zhao surrenders and goes back to his spot.

"Now, back to business. *Xíngshì.* I will make you *and* your mother suffer for your crimes."

He nods and the guard slams the key into Mama's cell door.

It *clicks* open.

I'm swept into the barren room. A shriveled figure lies in the corner, arms wrapped around herself. Her eyes are frozen in place, the fear in them raging.

She looks at Chen and then at me, shaking her head. My mouth drops a little and it won't close. Chen nods at a soldier and she slams the cell door shut.

"Lin, my rebellious wife—"

"*I am not your wife,*" Mama interrupts, her voice quivering slightly.

Her words crash into me. She hasn't sounded this strong since...forever. She sounds like her normal self again.

My heart beats happily for the first time but it drops once I take in my surroundings.

Chen's face turns into a fire. *"Don't. Talk. To. Me. Like. That.* You really were the worst of them all. No respect for your country, for your own husband. And worst of all, you spread your lies to your children. All of *this* has cost you *everything.*"

"Islam is not a 'this.' It's our religion and deserves as much respect as all other religions. Even if I have lost everything, I haven't lost the happiness of Allah. He will reward me for all my pain."

"*Enough.*" Chen barks. He reaches into his belt and rips his pistol out.

Click.

He loads his gun and the sound resonates throughout the cell. My breath lodges into my throat and refuses to exit.

"You will regret everything. *Everything.* If only you had listened. If only you had left your corrupt ways."

Chen aims the pistol to Mama's head. She gets up, standing until she is peering up into Chen's eyes.

"If I have to die, I should be an example for my daughter," she turns toward me, "Hala, never forget that I lov—"

Bam.

Bam.

Bam.

The deafening shots ring in my ears and Mama crumples to the ground. The bullets rip through her and lodge into the wall.

Splat.

Drops of red spray throughout the room. A few of them find my face and drip down but I can't move. A sea of blood spreads around her until she is drowning in crimson.

My knees lock and my feet glue themselves to the ground. Silent tears drip down my face, splatting into the growing blood river.

She's gone.

Gone.

Gone.

Gone.

And she's never coming back again.

A few soldiers file out of the room and others grip Mama's limbs, lifting her out of the room.

"Make sure I never see her again. Throw her into the sea if you have to," Chen murmurs.

My knees give in to the weight and I collapse onto the floor.

"Awww, the little girl wants her mama back," a guard mocks. Everyone, including Chen, laughs at me but their voices grow distant.

All I can hear are the

Bullets

Piercing

Mama's

Head

The tears flood out and my chest contracts as it struggles to breathe. The soldiers continue laughing, their deep voices buzzing.

"Enough," Chen booms and makes his way toward me, "Your punishment isn't over."

He nods to the guard next to him. "You know where to take her."

A knife plunges into my heart and when the soldier's hands grip my arm, I struggle. I thrash in his grip. "Let me go. Let me go."

But I'm weak.

I'm nothing compared to the man.

I stumble on the floor as the walls blur past me.

I continue struggling.

Doors open and slam shut.

I continue struggling.

The lights flicker and darkness takes over.

I continue struggling.

Until everything stops.

Creeeeaaak. Slam.

A heavy door shuts behind me and I'm in a small, white room.

An isolation room.

9

TOQQUZ

PANIC RUNS THROUGH my heart.

I thought Chen was going to kill me.

I thought that I was being led to an execution room.

The situation slowly descends onto me.

Chen doesn't want me dead. He wants me to suffer. He wants me to break. He wants me to feel pain.

But I'm not sure I have the courage to fight.

I'm not sure I have the courage to survive.

I sit down on the thin cot.

Thud. Thud. Thud.

Footsteps draw near and my heart beats in synchrony with them.

Creak.

The door throws itself open to reveal the tall man behind it.

"I see you've finally calmed down. You still have one more *rule* to follow before I leave you here."

Chen inches closer and reaches behind his back. Out come thick handcuffs.

Click.

He closes the chain around my wrist and attaches the other side to the bed frame.

"There, now everything is perfect."

He shuts the door behind him and it automatically locks.

It's just been a few hours but the loneliness is creeping into my mind. It consumes my thoughts like poison.

Mama's death lingers in my mind, even though I try to push it out. The shots ring in my ears, haunting my dreams and my thoughts. The way her bones collapsed crashes into me at random times.

I can't make it go away.

I can't get over it.

There's a hole in my heart that keeps on getting bigger and bigger.

Bzzzzzzz.

The speaker above comes to life.

Bam. Bam.

I shoot up, my eyes widening and my heart racing.

Bzzz.

"Did you really expect me to let you sit there? That's not enough,."

Bzzzzz.

Bam.

Bam.

Bam.

He wants me to suffer.

The realization hits me as Mama's execution plays again.

And again.

And again.

And again.

The cracking, the snapping, it never goes away.

Not as I sleep.

Not as I cover my ears.

Never.

I wrap the thin pillow around my ears but the volume just gets louder.

I should never have tried escaping.

I should have just accepted my fate.

I should have been thankful that I was not being punished.

But instead, I had to be foolish.

I had to risk others' lives.

Crack.

I sit up, my heart pounding against my bones.

"Who's there?" I peep.

Only silence greets me. Paranoia infects my mind.

Someone's here. Someone's watching me.

I remain sitting, my eyes scanning the room. A rush of adrenaline fuels my body and every nerve is tingling. My mind whispers,

Someone's there.

Someone's there.

Someone's there.

The shadows in the corner move, taking the shapes of people. They move closer and closer but once they're in the light, they retreat.

They're testing me out.

My eyes remain glued to the corner but a movement in the opposite direction catches my eye.

There are more.

They all advance together but retreat at the last second.

Again.

And again.

And again.

It never ends.

They never stop.

Until the sun sets.

I exhale deeply. *They're gone for the night. I can finally sleep.*

Crack.

I begin weeping internally and glare at the corner. The shadows are back, illuminated by moonlight.

I sit back up and resume glaring at the corner.

BZZZZ.

"Rise and shine," Chen yells through the speaker.

Bam.

Bam.

BAM.

I can feel the red cracks in my eyes and my brain feels numb. The world spins and the gunshots from above cause my heart to skip beats.

Crack.

Not again, I wail inside and bury my face into the pillow. I'll try going to sleep. If I can't see or hear them, they don't exist...

Right?

I close my eyes and my heart slows down. I'm drifting off into another world, the shots growing fader and fader.

Until I jerk awake.

"Who's there?" I shriek.

I scan the room but only silence greets me back. Someone tapped me on the shoulder. I know it. It was so...real. I couldn't have imagined that.

I dig my face back into the pillow and wrap everything around my body but the chills don't go away.

Someone or *something* continues to tap me.

Please go away. Please go away. Please. Please. Please.

But it doesn't.

I itch the urge to sit up because that person won't be there. They're too fast. Too smart.

As the tapping continues, my mind spirals into a tornado of confusion and terror until finally, I plummet into the darkness.

I wake up a few minutes later and jump out of bed. I jerk back as the chain tears at my wrist. Adrenaline surges through my veins as I analyze the room.

"Who's. There?"

No one responds.

What's wrong with me?

A realization dawns on me.

I can't continue living like this. I can't. Death is better. I'd rather be dead than here.

I peer around, searching for anything sharp but the room is stripped clean. I look at my wrists, gulp and bite down, watching as the red flows down my arms.

"MAMA? MAMA?" I shriek in the fog. A shadow runs toward me and Mama emerges from the white.

"Oh Hala," she cries and wraps her arms around me.

I cry into her shoulder. "I thought you were dead. I thought you were gone."

"I'm here now," she lifts my chin up, "I'll always be with you. Always."

"But you died in front of me. This...this is a dream."

She chuckles. "Even if it's a dream, it's something, right?"

I nod. We stay in that position for hours. A small cloud forms above us and it drizzles cool, refreshing rain. The splotches of blue, purple and red drip off my skin and the aches in my bones fade away.

My eyes widen in shock.

The pain...it's all gone. It's like it was never there. I look up into Mama's eyes and for the first time, I notice how happy she is. Her face glows and her eyes shine with tears of joy. Her skin shines and what used to be a bald head is replaced with a white scarf.

She smiles. "This is a much better place than where I was. I'm free from them. I'm free from Chen. Come with me, Hala."

For a moment, my heart leaps but a needle pricks it, injecting fear. "I...can't."

"Why?" she asks.

"I have to wait for Ürkesh. We'll go together."

A glass bead streams down Mama's cheek. "You passed the test. I knew you would."

She lets go of my hands, turns and begins walking away.

"Wait, Mama. Where are you going?"

She peers over her shoulder and her face is wet. "You passed the test. You made the right choice. But...you have to survive by yourself. I can't...go with you."

The dam in my eyes breaks open. "But you promised me,. You promised" I weep.

"I know but I have to go. You must complete your journey and get your brother back."

"You're leaving me alone?" I peep.

Her eyes crack red. "I have to," she says as she continues walking away.

Walking away from *me*.

I step forward and crash onto the grass. Ropes hold me back. "Nonono," I mutter but they only grow tighter.

I struggle but they

Don't

Let

Go.

My face is now a mess, my hair sticking to my cheeks. "Mama. Wait. Please," I shriek but she inches farther and farther.

"Please. Mama. WaitWaitWait," I scream at the top of my lungs but she doesn't turn around.

She continues walking

Farther

And

Farther

Away

Until she disappears into the sun.

I collapse onto the ground, my body twitching with each tear.

Mama left me. She's gone...again. She's not coming back.

The ropes loosen and retreat into the ground but I remain on the grass.

She's gone.

She's gone.

She's gone.

Uhhhhh.

I gasp awake and reach for my face. It's soaked wet.

It was just a dream. It was just a dream.

My heart stops pounding and I lay back down.

But...how did I fall asleep?

I lift my arms to my face and process the white clothes stuck to my wrists.

Who? When? Why?

I jump back to when I was biting at my wrists. Someone came in here when I had blacked out. But...who? Zhao? *Ürkesh?*

I begin to dream about the real Ürkesh coming back. We can escape together. We can finally get out of the country. We can live normally, away from this suffering.

Knock. Knock.

Knocking?

"May I come in," a muffled, male voice asks.

"Yes."

The door screams open as a tall man steps into the room. He holds a finger to his lips and points at my wrists.

I nod and mouth, *Thank you.*

Zhao breathes a sigh of relief but my heart continues dropping.

It wasn't Ürkesh.

Ürkesh doesn't remember.

We can't escape.

And I'm still stuck here.

Is everything alright, Zhao mouths.

I nod, even though it's not true.

He nods and closes the door behind him but my disappointment doesn't leave with him.

I peer at my wrists and a thought enters my head.

I can try again.

I push the thought out.

No, no. I promised Mama that I would stay for Ürkesh. I must fulfill my promise. I can survive this place. I can get my brother back.

I retreat into the corner and shove my thoughts into a bag. I hug my knees to my chest and rock back and forth. My eyes droop down and I'm about to fall asleep when deep voices lure me out of my trance.

"We're not knocking on the door. She's not a queen. She's a slave, a criminal," Chen yells.

The one he was talking to remains quiet and Chen storms to the door and throws it open. I shove my wrists behind my back.

"Yes, sir?" I mutter.

Chen analyzes me. "Have you learned your lesson?"

"Yes, sir. I will never disobey you again. I promise."

"*Hmmm,* I'll be kind to you this time but if you misbehave again, you'll be punished worse. Understand?"

I nod vigorously. Chen leaves the room and the door closes behind him. I try the knob.

It's unlocked.

I stick my head out of the door and Zhao gestures for me to get out. He waits as I cautiously emerge from the isolation cell.

"What time is it?" I ask Zhao.

"It's time for you to go to sleep. I'll convince Chen to let you have a few extra hours," he responds monotonously.

A tugging pulls at my heart. He's trying to make his betrayal up to me. He's trying to compensate for it.

We walk to my cell through a different hallway.

He's avoiding Mama's cell.

Creaaak.

Zhao nudges me into the cell and locks the door behind me. I stand close to the door and summon my courage from the pit of my stomach.

"Zhao?" I call.

"Yes?"

"You don't need to make it up to me. It's alright," I force the words out of my mouth because even though my tongue is saying this, my heart isn't.

A shadow covers his eyes and he opens his mouth to respond but nothing comes out.

"Really. It's alright. You did what you had to," I smile sadly at him.

Tears well up in his eyes and he turns around without saying a word. His footsteps echo throughout the hall until they abruptly stop.

"Chen..."

"Where is she?" Chen booms.

"She's in her cell," Zhao whispers.

"And how did she get there?"

"I let her in," he starts to beg, "Please, *Dìdì*, give her a break. Let her sleep for two more hours."

"Don't tell *me* what to do. I'm the leader here. That brat already sleeps enough. She doesn't need two extra hours."

"Please, sir. It's past ten. We both need rest and we won't be able to if the girl isn't in her cell," Zhao begins making excuses.

Chen remains silent for a few seconds as he glares at his brother. "Fine, fine but only this time. If you ask me for any more favors, I'll lock *you* in a cell."

"Yes, sir."

"Good, that's what I want to hear. Complete obedience. You were just so bad at being successful. Look where that took you," Chen mocks.

Zhao remains quiet and lets his brother bully him. I pinch the bridge of my nose. He should stand up to him. After all, Zhao is the older one. Why is he letting his younger brother bully him into submission?

Thud. Thud.

The footsteps grow crisp as they approach closer. Zhao takes a seat in his chair and reclines on it, staring aimlessly at the ceiling.

"You should stand up to him. He shouldn't abuse you like that. You're family," I say.

"I try but every time the words are in my throat, he finds exactly what to say to make them disappear."

"There's going to be a time when Chen will take things too far. What are you going to do then?"

"I'll say something then. Right now, I want to focus on surviving this place. Go to sleep before *Dìdì* wakes you up at one a.m."

He'll find out sooner or later.

I retreat to the corner closest to Mama's cell and lie there, expecting a word, a tear, a sound to come but it remains deathly silent.

She's not coming back. She's dead. Chen killed her. He even told the soldiers to throw her body into the ocean for all he cares. Why do you still expect her to be on the other side of the wall?

Without a second's thought, I respond. *Because hope is the only thing I have left.*

10

ON

DEEEEE. DEEEEEE

A sharp sound jolts me out of my sleep. I jump out of the corner and dart toward the door.

I rub my eyes and wait for the guard to open the door. The rest of the prisoners line up in front of the bathroom and I join them. The line inches closer and closer every minute until it's my turn.

"Your one minute starts now. Remember to use the water *correctly,*" the soldier barks.

I shut the door behind me, use the bathroom and wash my eyes with the water. We're not allowed to do anything else with the water or else we'll be beaten.

I examine myself in the cloudy mirror. A deep, brown gash runs across my face and my hair sprouts from random places. Patches of dirt cover my face and I try to rub them off but they're stubborn.

"Time's up," the soldier yells and I jump out of the bathroom. "Next time, I shouldn't have to remind you." She pats the metal rod in her belt.

"I'm sorry. It won't happen again," I apologize and run as far away as possible.

I throw open the door leading to the fields and soak in the warm sunlight. I breathe in the cool air.

I'm finally outside.

But the short moment of joy is overcome by a wave of grief.

Now, I'll be all alone. Everyone I've ever known is gone. I'm left to fend for myself.

I search around the area when I spot him.

Ürkesh.

I gaze at his stern face. Those eyes used to be playful and happy once. Now, they're full of hatred. That mouth was always pulled up into a smile but now, it hangs upside-down. His expression is like stone, no love, warmth or compassion.

If only you could come back.

Ürkesh's eyes turn to me and I look down.

Thud. Thud.

Thump. Thump.

My heart beats in synchrony with the thundering steps. "It doesn't seem like you're working," Ürkesh booms.

"I'm sorry, sir." I dare to glance up. Ürkesh's expression...softens? I tilt my head slightly.

"Hurry up and get to work," he says and moves out of the way. He leans into my ear. "I won't tell Father this time."

My eyes widen and I nod eagerly. I smile inside and run to the edge of the field. The white fluffs disappear into the sack as I rip them off, happy for the first time.

I stop moving my arms as a realization crashes into me.

It feels so good to be happy, to look forward to something exciting. Kindness feels so...nice. It's like I've been living in the darkness for a century, only to discover light. Is this what everyone else feels? Is this how the rest of the world is functioning?

Tap. Tap.

A touch on my shoulder rips me out of my world. "Excuse me, do you know Chen's son?" a man asks. The few hairs on his head are combed and his face is clean, except for the few specks of dirt.

My trust issues kick in. "I don't know what you're talking about," I lie.

"I saw you talking to the young man over there multiple times," his eyes point to Ürkesh, "It seems as if you know him."

"You must be confusing me for someone else."

"You don't need to lie to protect yourself. I'm not *them*. I'm not going to hurt you."

My heart slows down and I sigh. "Yes, he is...was my brother," I confess.

"So you're Chen's daughter?" A puzzled expression takes over his face.

The thought of that causes bile to climb my throat. *"No,"* I shriek before slapping my hand over my mouth. My eyes dart toward Ürkesh. "I'm sorry. He's my half-brother from my mom's side. We didn't know though. It was a hidden fact, something I was told recently."

"He was in Bao's camp, right?"

His words perk my ears up. "What? He was?"

He nods. "He looks exactly like the boy I saw in Bao's camp."

I look at Ürkesh and then back at the man. *"He* was in Bao's camp?"

"Yes, I'm sure of it. He was particularly close to the supervisor's assistant, Shan."

Ürkesh really was in Bao's camp but when? He couldn't have been there when I was.

"When was he there?" I ask.

"He came right after a girl was killed. She was pretty famous in the camp, leading an escape group and all. Anyway, after she was gone, he came into the camp. Bao targeted him, *a lot.* After two weeks or so, he managed to escape the camp and Bao went crazy. He vowed to kill every single one of us if the boy went on the news. After that, I was transferred here and I just noticed that Chen's son is the same child."

After a few moments of silence, the man speaks up again. "Doesn't he...seem a little different to you?"

A brick lodges into my throat. I nod. "He doesn't remember properly. Chen did something to him."

"Brainwashing. I never really believed they could do that."

"Do you know if it can be reversed in any way?" I blurt.

The man chuckles. "I don't know anything about the Chinese's torture methods. I've just heard what the people say. But if you want my advice, *Háizi,* no one can take away what you love. If your brother loves you, he will remember. There's always a way."

I nod, taking in his words. "Thank you for your kindness, uncle."

"You're welcome," he turns to leave but stops. He looks down toward my feet. "It's only fair that I tell you something about myself. I've always wanted children but now...that doesn't seem possible."

The man leaves without saying another word, lost in his thoughts. My heart aches for him. He went out of his way to give me information about Ürkesh, information I need to piece together the gap.

But he's right. Ürkesh will remember. I just have to make him remember.

BZZZ.

The lights shut off and darkness settles in. Every movement echoes through the hall as whispers travel through cells.

"Blackout."

"Blackout."

"Blackout."

The darkness also provides cover. Everything is down. The cameras, the locks, everything. I lie awake in the corner, watching every single movement.

The guards come and go as the hours tick by. Once the shadows wander around the corner and the halls are deserted, I slip the key out of my pocket.

Guilt pulls at my heart. I stole the key from Zhao. If I get caught, he'll get in trouble.

The scene plays again.

I inch toward the end of the hallway, the echoing footsteps getting louder and louder. I exhale, closing my eyes. I step forward and smash, I collide into someone.

A hand reaches for my shoulder.

"Are you alright?" a soft voice asks.

I nod and Zhao continues walking.

I glance at the key in my hand.

I take a deep breath.

Click.

The key slides in place and the door *creeaaks* open. I scan the area, peering into every crevice and step out of the sanctuary of my cell.

I glue myself to the wall and cautiously approach the end of the hallway. Still no one in sight.

Click.

The looming door slides open, revealing another hall. A few turns later, the biggest door lies ahead of me, laughing.

Click.

The door cackles and a gust of cool wind brushes my hair. The feeling of freedom is so refreshing, so enlivening.

You don't have enough time. You must focus. Focus on your task, your mission.

I take a deep breath of fresh air and my legs begin moving in circles. I tumble into the bushes and wait.

If I planned everything correctly, Chen will be coming out...right now.

A light flickers in the building before extinguishing. A figure emerges from the door, locks it and enters into his car.

Vrrrmm.

The car gasps awake and flies down the abandoned, dusty road. I run after it, trying to monitor its turns but soon, it disappears into the night sky.

Around me, mounds of dirt fly by. After a few minutes, they fade into towering trees, their branches reaching out.

Now's your chance. You can run away. You can be free. Hurry before it's too late.

I push the thoughts away. I must get to Ürkesh. There has to be a way to revive his former self. There has to be.

I continue sprinting to the edge of the road and listen for the exhausted car. I turn to the right, then to the left and left again before the car dies. A cluster of houses lay isolated, the bustling city's lights flying through the sky. Chen's car lies exhausted in the corner house and when I place my hand on the hood, it snorts.

I look up at the massive house with elaborate windows. Its front door is made of expensive wood...I don't know exactly what type of wood but it *looks* expensive, at least.

The house's roof is defined by tiny dragons carved onto it and wide beams hold it up.

I've arrived.

I've arrived at Chen's house.

11

ON BIR

I HIDE OUT in the plants around Chen's house and wait.

And wait

And wait

The lightbulbs around the house turn on and off in a pattern. Seconds, minutes and hours pass by. My legs burn and my back grows stiff but I continue waiting. Fear and doubt trickle into my heart.

As if on cue, the light upstairs goes out and silence spreads throughout the house. I wait for a few more minutes before circling it.

There must be an unlocked window or door. Something, anything.

I lightly rattle all the entry points and *crack,* one of the windows moves. I push it up and it slides open. I peer left and right and enter the forbidden house.

I tip-toe across the hallways until a large doorway comes into sight. I try the door and it opens, revealing the large office area. In the center lies a massive, wooden desk and on the walls, bookshelves are flooded with books.

I sneak in closer to take a closer look at the books.

China.

CCP.

Xi Jinping.

All of them are about China and its greatness.

Focus. You have to find what you're searching for.

I instantly jump to the desk and try the drawers.

Locked.

Frustrated, I rummage through the papers and gadgets on the desktop.

Clink.

A metallic object crashes onto the floor. I freeze, taking in all the sounds. After a minute, I breathe. No one woke up. I pick the key up and jam it into the hole.

Click.

As the drawer slides open, my eyes see them first.

Our passports.

I pick Mama's up and examine her young, shining face. Ürkesh is next, smiling as a young boy and finally, mine. My hands hold the closed book and I stuff all three of them into my pocket.

I can't look at my passport because I'm afraid of what I'll see.

I'm afraid of getting too hopeful.

I'm afraid of losing that hope.

As I sit thinking, a dark object in the back of the drawer catches my eye. I reach for it and when it becomes clear in the moonlight, I stuff it into my pocket as well.

Creeeeeeak.

The floor groans sharply and I freeze. The door slowly opens, revealing a tall, male figure.

NoNoNo.

I duck under the desk, gripping my legs to my chest and hold my breath. The slow, careful footsteps draw closer and closer until they're right in front of me.

"Hmm," the figure wonders and closes the open drawer. He ruffles through the desk's content and stops. He backs up and examines the rest of the room, searching into every corner and hiding place.

Please don't look down. Please don't look down. Please. Please. Please.

Sounds pierce the silent, tense air as the figure continues looking. Objects move and papers rustle until he returns to the desk.

My breath burns in my lungs and it begs to be let out. It makes its way up and erupts from my mouth.

The figure gasps and glances down. My eyes widen as he stares at me.

Crash.

The man runs to the corner and *flash,* the light explodes on. The white blinds my eyes and everything is a blur. Immediately, I'm swept off the ground and my feet thrash violently in the air.

As the color begins to return, my captor's face grows clear.

Ürkesh.

12

ON IKKI

MY HEART BEGINS to pound.

"I...Ürkesh."

"What. Are. You. Doing. Here."

"Listen to me—"

"I *warned* you that next time I would tell Father. This is our home and you think you *Bèndàn* can just sneak in? Don't worry, don't you worry." He drags me to the office door. "This is the last thing you'll ever do. *I'll get rid of you myself."*

"Ürkesh...Ürkesh," I pant as I continue stumbling after him, "Please, give me a chance. Let me explain."

"My name is not Ürkesh," he roars and throws me onto the floor. I scramble to get back on my feet but he pounces.

Thwack. Thwack.

He strikes me on the face, my skin tingling from his blows. The pain radiates through my jaw and tears form in my eyes.

"Let go," I croak.

"No. Father will be proud of me for this."

"He won't. He'll never be proud. He'll never love you like a son. You're only a *thing* to him, an object to be used."

"You're a liar just like the rest of your kind. Father doesn't abuse anyone. Everyone else is just inferior to him. They just aren't as strong, as successful, as brave as he is," he boasts.

"Do you hear yourself? Praising *Chen?*"

Slam.

Ürkesh smashes me against the wall and a wet river streams down my face.

Drip. Drip.

It falls to the ground, painting it crimson. He pants like an animal and readies himself to hit me again.

In those few seconds, time slows. I can see every muscle move in his body. I reach into my pocket and snatch the object in it. I hold my hands in front of my face, close my eyes and wait for the impact.

It doesn't come.

I slowly open my eyes to find Ürkesh staring at it, still as a statue. Something different shines in his eyes and a battle between the red and blue commences,

Until the red overshadows the blue and he raises his fist again.

I brace myself and let the words flow.

"No matter how much you hurt me, you are still my brother and I will always love you."

I watch as his eyes return to their confused, cool state. His eyes widen as everything surges back.

"Ürkesh?"

"Be quiet. Be quiet. Leave me alone."

He turns around to face the wall and grasps his head.

"What...What is that?" he asks softly.

"It's your *doppa*. Mama gave it to you as a gift and you used to wear it all the time."

"Wh...Where is she now?" he murmurs.

The world freezes.

Ürkesh is back.

The words bounce through my heart.

"Somewhere safe," I whisper.

All the grief,

All the pain,

All the despair floats away.

Ürkesh

Is

Back.

I embrace my brother for the first time after all those minutes,

All those days,

All those months of separation.

"But...Hala...what happened? What am I doing in Chen's house?" he whispers.

"He brainwashed you."

His jaw drops, revealing the black inside. Sorrow paints his eyes. He points at the bruise on my forehead. "I must have done that," he mutters.

"Don't worry about it. Really."

All that matters is that we're together.

For now... an eerie voice hisses in my head.

I shake my head and the words flutter away.

"Hala, I'm so...I can't—"

Thud.

    Thud.

        THUD.

            THUD.

"Someone's coming. Hide." Ürkesh shoves the *doppa* into my arms, pushes me under the desk and slams the drawers shut.

"What's going on here," Chen yawns.

"Nothing, Father. I was hungry and went downstairs to grab something. I saw that your office's light was on and was going to turn it off." Ürkesh rests his hand on the light switch.

"I must have left it on by mistake. I'm proud of you for taking the initiative, son."

Ürkesh beams. "Your pride is all I want, Father."

Chen smirks. "Well, since you're awake, do you mind cleaning my office a bit? I haven't had time this week."

"Yes, Father."

"I'm going back to sleep. I have a long day tomorrow," Chen trudges up the stairs.

Ürkesh shoves papers into drawers and books onto their shelves in silence. After a few minutes, when snoring can be heard from upstairs, he crouches down.

"What should we do?" I ask.

"I don't—*Uff*," Ürkesh slams his head against the desk. He rubs his forehead as a paper flies down. He grabs it and soaks the words.

"I think we should stay," he mutters.

"Stay? We can literally walk out of this place and leave China," I whisper sharply.

He hands me the paper and I read it.

Mr. Fu,

I hope I can trust you with these documents. These are incredibly confidential and should not be seen by anyone but you. The security of the nation depends on you.

I look up at Ürkesh. "This...this isn't our concern. We should run while we can."

"Hala, these documents could be the proof that we need. We can save everyone with them. There are so many of us that have escaped but no one is listening. No one will unless we give them solid proof."

"And how do you plan to get them?"

He thinks carefully and a blanket of silence descends. "I'll pretend to still be brainwashed and get my hands on those documents."

"No. It's too dangerous. We need to leave now."

You know he's right. You know you want to help. You know it's the right thing to do.

"Hala, you have to listen. Even if we leave, everyone else will still be here. Everyone else will still be dying. We need those documents and we have easy access to them."

"Even if you do get your hands on those documents, we can't keep them. That will make Chen suspicious," I say.

"We can take pictures. I can find something to take them with."

A lightbulb flashes above my head. "The phone."

"What phone?"

"I found Mama's phone in Kazakhstan and hid it. We can use that," I grin.

Ürkesh smiles wearily. "Okay but we have to be as secretive as possible. Don't tell anyone."

I nod and we sit in silence for a few seconds. Ürkesh gets up. "Come on. I'm not sending you back before you eat," he says.

"Eat?"

The word seems foreign.

"I told Chen I was up for a midnight snack for a reason. He'll never suspect it. I'll bring something. Stay under the desk."

He turns the light off and gently closes the door. His shadow retreats farther and farther until it disappears. A warm feeling spreads through my blood.

I've missed him so much. It's been so long since we last saw each other.

He comes back into the office but keeps the light off. His arms are overflowing with food. My mouth fills with water and the monster in my stomach growls in satisfaction.

I devour everything, not caring if it's freezing cold and once I'm done, I burp. I cover my mouth shamefully.

"I'm not a stranger. I'm your brother. You can burp in front of me," Ürkesh grins.

"It's still embarrassing though." I gently punch him in the shoulder.

He chuckles but something's holding him back. "What's wrong?"

"Nothing, nothing," he shakes his head, "Did you eat enough?"

"Yep. Plenty. I haven't eaten in so long."

He stares at the clock. "It's getting late. I think you should go."

"But..."

"Chen will be awake soon. It'll be too late then. We'll never be able to make it out if you don't go back."

He walks out of the office and I follow him out without saying a word. He opens the door and I walk back out into the darkness. He quietly shuts the door behind him and I can hear his steps going up the stairs and into his room. After that, complete silence.

Instantly a hole forms in my heart. I just found my brother and I lost him again.

I've never felt so empty,

So cold,

So alone.

Now, we're risking our lives to prove to the world that we're in trouble.

That we've been forgotten.

That we've been abandoned.

And maybe we'll never be able to get out of China, out of these camps. Maybe our lives were meant to be lived here. Maybe it's destiny for us to go extinct, for all of humanity to forget that we even exist.

I retrace my footsteps back to the dusty road,

Back to the dark camp,

Back to the unlocked camp gate,

Back into my lonely cell.

This time the hallways aren't silent. Zhao is lazily asleep in his chair, his feet up on the desk to support his long legs. He's left the cell door open.

My heart is too empty to think. I step back into my cell, lock the door and try to rest in the corner. But my thoughts keep the sleep away.

"WAKE UP," I hear a voice calling out. My eyes flutter open to see a blurry figure standing near the door. "Chen will be back soon. I don't want him to target you."

I force myself to get off the stone floor and Zhao opens the cell for me. Outside, the sun's barely peeking out, the streaks of blue and black still evident among the red and yellow rays. The hallways are still dark, no sign of life among them.

Deeee. Deee.

The sharp noise pierces my ears and I jump, even though it's been a few weeks since I've arrived at this camp.

I'm still not willing to accept reality.

I'm still not willing to accept the suffering.

I drag myself to the outskirts of the field where not a single soul remains. It's where me and Mei used to talk. Where it felt like I actually had a friend for the first time. But even that was taken away.

She was taken away because of me.

Because I didn't think everything through.

Mama is gone because of me too. Chen wouldn't have killed her if it wasn't for me. If I would just accept the situation, people would stop dying because of me.

It's not your fault. None of this is your fault and you know that. Stop telling yourself that you're responsible and that everyone's dying because of you. It's their fault. Stop lying to yourself.

I want to argue but I can't. I don't have the energy. The shadow at the opposite side of the field forces me to pull away from my thoughts.

Ürkesh.

The events of last night unfold in front of me. It doesn't feel real. I can't believe it. Doubts begin to creep into my mind.

Stop.

That one word causes every single shadow in my mind to vanish. I watch carefully as he creeps closer and closer and closer, until he is right in front of my eyes. Ürkesh peers side to side until he's finally satisfied that no one else is around. The stern look on his face softens as a sense of security watches over him.

"Where's the phone?" he asks, getting straight to the point.

"I...I forgot to get it. But we need a way to get those documents close enough to the phone. Then we need to find a way to hide the phone in a safer place, just in case, you know..." my speech trails off.

My brother squeezes my shoulder. "I know you're afraid. I know you want to get out of here but this is also important. Without proof, no one's going to believe us. There are plenty of people who escaped the camps but no one does anything about it because China always finds a way to cover it up. With this hard proof, it's going to be impossible for everyone to ignore us."

"I know, I know, I keep telling myself that too but it's still difficult not to be afraid, not to fear that we will never make it out of here."

Ürkesh smiles brightly. "This doesn't sound like the Hala I knew."

That hits me and I immediately scold myself.

What's wrong with me? I wasn't like this when I was in Bao's camp. This is new. Chen isn't scarier than Bao. They're basically twins. I don't have anything to be afraid of.

I look up at Ürkesh and slightly smile. He smiles back. Suddenly, fear takes over his eyes and the coldness returns.

Crunch. Crunch.

"What's going on here?" Chen asks.

"Nothing, Father. I just want to keep an eye on this troublemaker," Ürkesh responds, his scowl growing deeper. He glances back at me. "Get back to work. You don't have a single second to waste."

My nerves kick in and I turn toward the plants, taking them off their sprouts.

"You're going to be a great supervisor one day, just like me."

"I can never be like you, Father. You are one of a kind."

Chen smirks. "You really know how to stroke your father's ego. Well, I'll let you do your work. Call me if you're having trouble with this one."

"Yes, sir."

Chen turns around, growing smaller and smaller on the horizon. Ürkesh finally breathes.

"Make sure to get the phone. In that time, I'll search for the documents," he says right before walking away.

Once I'm alone, the silence sinks in. *I don't want to be alone anymore. Paranoia settles in when no one is around. I grow anxious and I begin to doubt everything. I hate living here. I want to leave.*

My mind wanders to the electronic device that could save all of us.

I need to get to it. The faster we take the pictures, the faster we get out of here.

I creep closer to the main area, picking cotton at the same time. Once I fill my second bag, I put it on my shoulder and drop it next to the factory building.

Hmmmm. Hmmm.

Distant whispers perk my ears up and I step forward to find the source.

Mind your own business. You don't need to put your life on the line because someone is whispering.

But everything that is talked about here involves everyone, including me. I need to know to protect myself.

I peek around the corner to find Chen and Ürkesh standing there. Chen's back is to me while he talks.

"I'm proud of you for keeping an eye on that troublesome slave. What I'm going to tell you must be kept between the two of us," Chen warns.

"You can trust me, Father."

"That girl looks like she's always planning something. She has this fire in her eyes that never goes away. She's going to cause me a lot of problems. I need to find a way to get rid of her but I can't without an excuse."

Ürkesh's eyes wander slightly until they lock with mine. He shakes his head a little bit and beckons for me to leave.

No, I mouth.

"Kai, Kai?" Chen waves a hand in front of Ürkesh's eyes.

"Oh, sorry, yes?" he stammers.

"What were you staring at?"

Chen turns to peek behind him and I duck behind the wall.

"Nothing. I was just thinking about..."

"About?" Chen urges on.

"I don't want you to experience any trouble. You don't deserve that. You've worked so hard to get here" Ürkesh croaks.

Chen smiles. "You need to keep an eye on that girl so we can make sure that never happens."

Ürkesh salutes. "Yes, sir."

"Good. We've got to keep her suppressed. She caused Bao a lot of trouble. We don't want trouble here."

Both of them nod and go in opposite directions. I run to the factory area, grab another bag and dart into the field.

But I wasn't fast enough.

"Why weren't you listening to me? It's dangerous. You shouldn't be spying on our conversations," Ürkesh scolds.

"It's necessary for me to know what Chen talks about."

"No, it's not," he sighs, "Hala, it's not your job to know everything. You can't save everyone. You must protect *yourself* first, then others. It's survival of the fittest, not survival of the most caring."

"Yeah but—"

"No buts. You *can't.* If you try, you'll be sacrificing the both of us. If you go down, I go down as well. You need to accept reality."

A rock forms in my throat and I nod.

"Hurry and start working before Chen grows more suspicious than he already is."

"Okay," is all I manage to say. Ürkesh's eyes grow sad but we both know he's right.

'See, I told you—'

I tuck my inner voice away. I can't listen to it right now.

The rest of the day passes by like this, in silence and sadness. But even then, one thing keeps me going forward.

The phone.

KHHHAAAA. KHHAAAA.

Zhao's snores echo throughout the cell, driving the sleep away. Sleep hasn't been coming for a long time. I've been waiting for the silence.

I inch back and *creeeeaaak,* the pot screams. Zhao stirs a bit and I freeze, my hand trembling. He relaxes and continues snoring.

I lift the pot up and reach around. My finger brushes the cool screen and I grip the device.

Crash.

I drop the phone and sit up, pressing against a wall. A tall shadow inches closer and closer as my heart beats faster and faster. I hug my knees and hold my breath.

Crash.

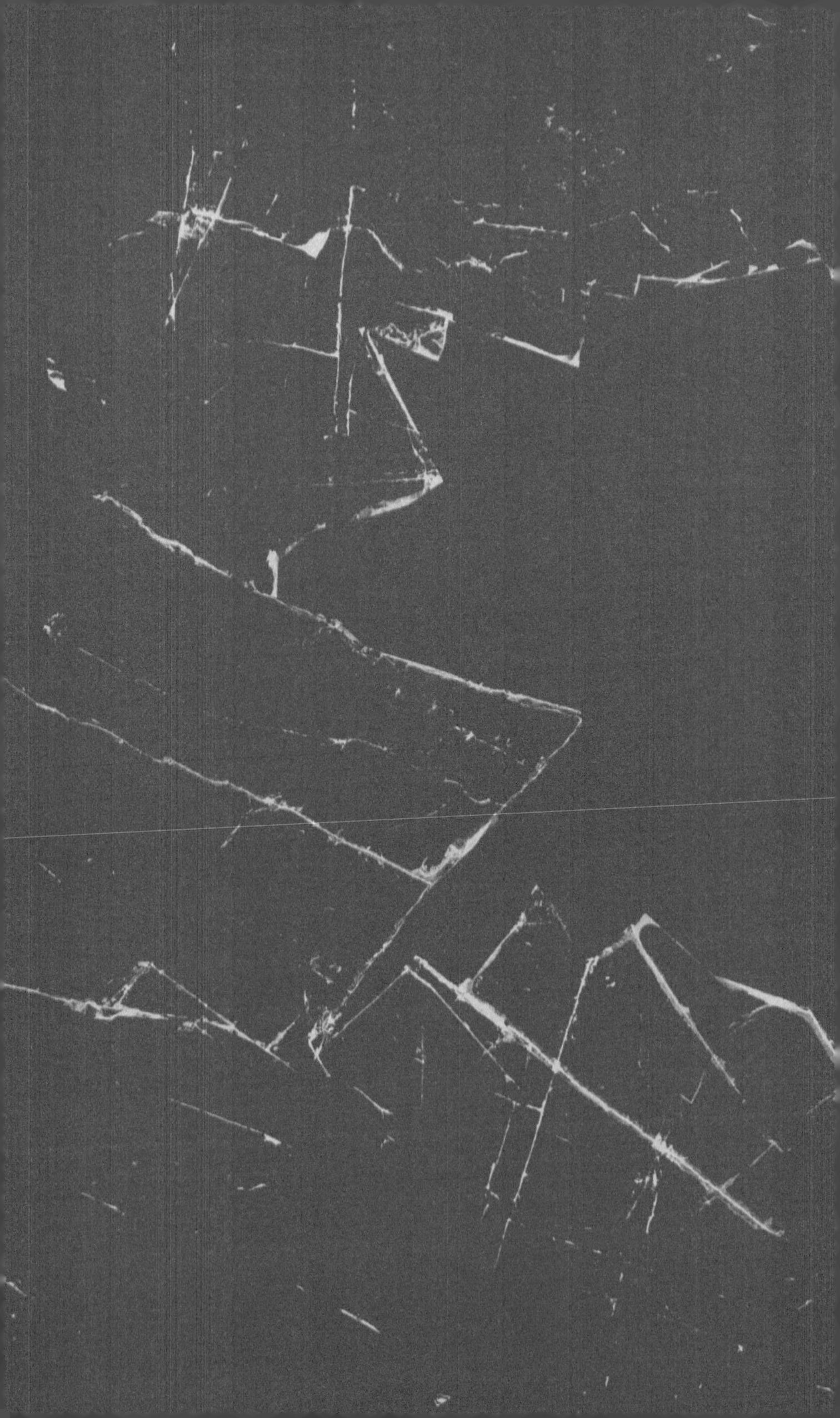

ÜRKESH

XINJIANG

NOW

13

ON ÜCH

I GRAB CHEN by his shoulders and heft him up. He swings a weak punch but ultimately collapses onto the floor.

I tip-toe to Hala's cell and mouth, *It's fine.*

She nods, lets herself go and grabs the phone from under her. A rush of calmness streams through me.

This will provide the proof we need to stop all th—

Chen mumbles something inaudibly and I remember what I'm doing here. I throw his arm over my shoulder and hold him up.

I strain under the weight. "You have to walk."

"Walk," he hiccups, "What's that?"

I grumble. "Place your left foot—no your other foot—no don't collapse—Che...Father, you have to—"

He falls onto me and I barely hold him up.

"Stand up before we both fall down," I croak.

"Haha, fall down. That sounds fun," he chuckles.

"No, it's not fun. Yes, yes, yes. There you go. Now, place this foot over there. Now that foot over there. See, you got it."

"Where's the car?" I ask.

"Car? Oh, at hoooooome. When are we going to sleep?"

"We first have to walk home."

"Walk? Why walk?"

"Because you left the car at home. Nonono. Step. Yes, like that. Just like that."

It's going to be a long night.

THE WALK TOOK two hours, even though it should have taken less than thirty minutes. We crash into the house and I throw Chen on the sofa.

My legs wobble from holding Chen's weight and my back is stiff. Outside, the night sky is still murky with only a few rays coming out of the moon.

I sit down at the edge of the stairs and rest my head against the wall. A chilly gust of wind blows through the window and I force myself up to close it.

I sit back down.

It's okay if I close my eyes for one minute. It doesn't harm anyone.

I shut my eyes and allow my mind to wander the universe.

WHITE LIGHT TICKLES my face and my eyes flutter open. Chen groans in the corner but doesn't wake up. The sofa creaks as he turns.

The curtains are wide open, light flooding in. I lift my head off the wall, stretch and yawn.

What time is it?

I trudge to the kitchen and glare at the number staring back at me.

7:16 a.m.

I jerk and dash toward the front door. I jump into my shoes.

I'm late. So, so late. Hala must be expecting me. Everyone must be expecting me. Everyone must be expecting *Chen.*

A weight pulls my heart down. I don't know if I can keep this up. I don't know how much longer I can pretend. I don't even know if Chen even believes my act. For all I know, he could be toying with me.

The towering, metal gates inch closer and closer as my steps grow heavier and heavier. Two white towers sprout from either side of the gate, two armed soldiers at the top. Around the gate is a concrete wall, barbed wire spiraling on top.

At the gate, guards stand ready with rifles slung over their shoulders.

"ID?" a guard asks.

I nod and search my pockets.

No, it's not there.

I pat my shirt.

No, it's not there.

I dig in my pockets again.

No. It's not there.

"You should be able to identify me without an ID, right? You should know who I am," I say.

"I'm sorry, sir. I need to see an ID in order to let you in. It's the government's rules, not mine. See, if it were up to me, I would let you in b...but I can't. Are you sure you don't have it?"

I pat my pockets again. "No, I don't. There's absolutely no way you can let me in?" I ask.

"I'm sorry. I can't," he leans in to whisper into my ear, "Please don't tell Chen. He'll kill me. I'm just following orders."

I gulp and steel my voice. "Now, I'm going to have to walk back home and then here. That's a few miles *in the sun.* My father deserves to know about this, right?"

The guard's face drops. "Well...Uh...I mean..."

"I'll be on my way now," I say.

"Hey, umm...Kai, you weren't serious about telling your father, right?" The guard chuckles nervously.

My stomach churns. "Did it seem like I was joking?" I reply, gritting my teeth.

"I'm really sorry, sir. I'm just following orders, the government's rules. If I was in charge, I wouldn't make these silly laws. Please, don't tell your dad."

I shrug. "I'll have *plenty* of time to think about it during the walk."

An hour later, I drag myself back to the camp gate and flash my ID. The guard beams artificially. "Thank you, kind sir. You will be the next great."

I glance at my watch. *8:52 a.m. Hours since my was supposed to start.*

The lights around me fly by as the hallway twists and turns. Groups of soldiers laugh in the corner, straightening up when I pass by. The instant I leave, they continue laughing and joking.

I step out the door into the sunlight. I take a deep breath of fresh air and let the breeze tickle me. My eyes scan the sprouts of green for my sister.

She's not here. She's supposed *to be here.*

I sigh when I remember who my sister is.

She never lets rules confine her. She's probably out there, doing someone else's work or nursing someone to health. That's her strength, helping others. She wants to save everyone, even if it means sacrificing herself. It'll kill her one day.

I turn back toward the door. Inside, the prisoners' arms begin moving faster. Their backs stiffen as I pass by. My eyes stick to them as my body goes the opposite way.

Crash.

I slam into a rock but the hand on my shoulder tells me otherwise. I rub my eyes and stare up into Zhao's sad eyes.

"Where is prisoner 98?"

"I haven't memorized everyone's numbers yet," he replies.

"My *supposed* sister."

"She's in the factory," he mutters.

I pretend to be irritated. "Who sent her to work there? She's assigned to the fields."

"Your father did. He left a note stating that she has been transferred to the factories. I don't know the reasoning behind it."

I nod coldly and spin back around. I scan each head in front of me.

No, no, no, no, n—there.

Hala dumps spools of thread into a box. She meets my eyes for a split second before turning around. I swim through the crowds of people before I make it. I glance from side to side but everyone is absorbed in their work.

Where is it, I mouth.

She slips her hand into a box and brings out the phone.

I stuff it into my pocket and make my way to Chen's office.

"Where are you going?" A sharp voice calls out from beside me. I turn to look straight into a soldier's eyes. "I see your father's not here."

"He's not coming today," I mutter back.

"So no one can save you now, right?" A sly grin spreads on his face.

At that moment, I search him up and down. He seems...familiar. He's tall, with grayish eyes. A shallow scar runs across his nose and lips.

I have to play the part. "You dare talk to me like that? Wait until I tell your supervisor."

He blocks my way and shoves me back. "You won't be telling Chen anything." The man slams his fist into his palm. I back up slightly.

"Oh, are you afraid? Are you afraid of a soldier?" he mocks.

I straighten my back and look into his eyes. I curl my hands into fists, my muscles tense. The man steps forward.

"Is there a problem?" A tired voice calls out from the hallway.

Zhao.

The man lowers his fists and salutes him. His jaw twitches. "No, sir."

Zhao's expression hardens. "If I were you, I wouldn't mess with him. Then, you would have to deal with the *three* of us. Understand?"

The man nods vigorously, scowls at me and disappears into the darkness.

"If Jie does that again, call me. We can't have him causing trouble here," Zhao says.

I nod, trying to keep my stone-like expression from collapsing. I put my hand against my pocket, just to make sure the phone is still there.

My nerves tingle and I glance back to find Hala glaring at me. *It's okay,* I mouth but her concerned look doesn't evaporate. Her face is bleached a ghostly white and her mouth hangs agape.

I flash a quick smile and drag myself out into the hallway. Some lights flicker with electricity buzzing. Most of the cells are empty, only the sickly left to rot in them.

A bloodcurdling scream erupts from beside me. A thick, metal door blocks me from the site and the screams turn into pleading. The world begins to spin.

"No, no, no, please, please. Pleasepleaseplease. I'll do anything. Please."

"No. Shut. Up. You thugs don't know how to respect those superior to you. You can only be taught with the whip."

The woman continues begging, pleading, as if the words went right through her head, having no impact.

Crack. Crack.

"Even the whip doesn't teach you manners. There is only one more way left and believe me, it is the worst."

"No. No. Please. Ple—"

Slush.

Slush.

Slush.

Slush.

"You dogs are useless. You all deserve to be killed. You were made for that very reason."

I crash back into reality and put a hand over my chest. My heart pounds like a drum, beating more and more intensely.

'This happened a long time ago,' The Voice tries to comfort.

But it doesn't work.

What was that? When did that happen? Why don't I remember?

'The *doppa* didn't release all your memories yet. It'll take some time. In the meantime, you will have gaps in your memory. You need to keep on going. Focus on your task.'

I continue walking down the hallways but the agonizing screams continue ringing in my ears.

Restricted.

The red sign screams out as if it's calling my name. This is it. This is the place.

I bend down to look at the knob. There isn't a key hole but an electronic lock. I glance at my ID and then at the dark gray block with the glaring red light. I press the card against the light and it transforms into green. The door *clicks* open, hissing as I cautiously enter.

14

ON TÖT

THE SMELL HITS me like a punch to the nose.

Alcohol.

This is where Chen must have been drinking. A chill settles in my bones. Chen could've done anything to Hala if I hadn't come. He could've killed her. He could've—

'Well, that didn't happen. There's no use dwelling on what *could have* happened. However, what *can* happen right now is getting caught,' The Voice interrupts.

I glance over my shoulder and step behind the desk. Countless drawers and cabinets cover the walls, labels on each one.

Records.

Interrogation.

Passports.

Confidential.

I tug on the drawer but it remains stuck.

Of course, they're locked.

I ruffle through the papers on top but there's nothing. I look at the desk.

Nothing.

I clutch my head but the answer doesn't come.

Thud.

My heart jumps at the sound and I bolt out of the office. Once I'm a hundred steps away, I glance behind me. The air in my lungs escapes and I lean against a wall.

Where does Chen keep the key? As I'm sucked into my own world, countless guards pass by, saluting me. I continue staring at the ceiling, as if the answer will drop onto me.

Clink. Clink.

I straighten up and look toward the sound. On a passing soldier, a ring of keys jingles.

Of course.

Every soldier has keys. Chen must have one too. That's where the key is.

"Aren't you supervisor of the day?" a mouse-like voice calls out.

I turn to find the hostile man from earlier glaring at me.

"Me?" I ask.

"Yes, you. Who else could I be talking to? Seems like you're not doing your job."

"I *am* working. You soldiers just don't understand."

"Really? Well, if you're *working,* you should keep an eye on these workers. They aren't going to guide by themselves."

I nod, the words 'yes, sir' almost rolling off my tongue. He scans me with fiery eyes.

What have I ever done to get this soldier's hatred?

The rest of the day passes by like this. I wander around the building, nodding at guards. Every time I look at them, my heart stops.

I step outside and gaze at the scene before me. A few figures are bent over, picking cotton. Above, streaks of blue and black paint the sky. Little white dots cover the darkness and watch as the moon climbs higher and higher.

A figure steps beside me and leans back against the wall. "You can go home, if you want," Zhao says.

I turn toward him. "Doesn't Che—Father's shift end in a few more hours?" I respond.

"I can take care of it from here. It's my job to get everyone into their cells. It isn't difficult," his voice becomes hushed, "and a child like you shouldn't be here."

My head perks up but he doesn't notice. "Are you sure?"

He nods. "Thank you," I say.

I rush out of the camp gates, eyeing the stationed guards' rifles. They salute me as I pass by. The black land ahead of me cackles and dares for me to come forward.

The camp lights grow fuzzy in the distance and with each step, I sink deeper and deeper into terror.

Anyone can be watching. Anyone can be waiting.

My walk turns into a gallop and then a run. The rubble around me flies by as my lungs burn.

But I keep on going.

Faint lights call out to me in the distance. Soon, a small cluster of houses come into sight.

Smash.

I storm through Chen's front door. The sofa *creaks* and a blanket ruffles. "Kai? Is that you?" Chen calls out.

"Yes, Father." I grip my knees and steady my breathing.

In. Out. In. Out.

I walk down the wooden hallway and into the living room. Chen lies on the sofa with his feet up, a book cracked upon in his lap. On the marble side table, there's a cup of juice and noodles. A red blanket is curled up at his feet.

I sit down in the leather chair in front of him. He glances toward me and then continues reading.

'You have to keep up the good son act,' The Voice reminds me.

I take a deep breath. "What are you reading?" I ask.

"A book on how the Chinese government is necessary for Uyghur survival. It's a great book. Try it some time," he says.

A question chews at me. "I will...Father?"

"Yes?"

"I have a question."

Chen puts his book down and sits up. "Alright."

"Why were you drinking? Don't weak men drink?"

Chen leans forward, locking his hands together, and slouches forward.

"Everyone has problems, Kai, and it's during tough times that a person's true strength is revealed. I've...just had too much to handle. You don't remember this but you had a half-brother, Liang. Some things happened and he died a few months back. My wi—*former* wife divorced me after that. A few weeks later, I found someone who was perfect. Someone who understood me. Someone who cared. The wedding was scheduled for next week."

Chen chuckles sadly and he sits there, staring into nothingness. "She...canceled it. She found out about Liang's death, about how my anger got the best of me. She told me...she told me that she doesn't want anything to do with me. She didn't want anything to do with an angry man."

We sit in tense silence.

"Everyone expects me to be strong, to be emotionless but it's just not possible. I'm human. I get hurt. I feel things."

We're humans too, just like you.

Chen sighs and puts his face in his hands. If I was a great actor, I would have gone over to him and comforted him.

But I can't.

I can't because he's hurt me.

I can't because he's hurt Hala.

I can't because he's hurt us all.

Chen remains like that while the heavy air shoves me out of the room. I trudge up the stairs, absorbed in my head.

Crash.

I grab my throbbing nose and the wall in front of me grows crisp.

How did I crash into a wall?

I glance to my left to find a cracked-open door. I tip-toe toward it and stick my head through the gap.

My jaw drops.

Inside, a gigantic bed lies there, surrounded by two side tables. A wide TV is mounted on the wall with a dark, wooden dresser underneath. Lace curtains frame the window.

I bounce to the next room, which is the bathroom. Even that is luxurious. The floor is covered in marble tiles and the faucets look like they're made of gold. The shower is as big as a room, with a seat.

I peel my eyes off and move over to the next room. This one is different from the others. A small bed lies on the side, covered in dark blue covers. On the opposite side, there's a desk with books neatly piled on the side. A corkboard hangs above the desk, pictures plastered on every inch.

I step forward to examine them. A skinny boy, about my age, smiles in each one.

"Took you long enough," I complain to the shadow.

Click.

The cell door shrieks open and a tall, bony boy comes into view.

"I'm sorry. Father didn't go to sleep early. That's why it took me a little longer."

I hug him. "I was just teasing you."

He laughs quietly. "Here," he hands me a small, cloth bag. I open it up and my mouth waters. I rip the fruit out and stuff it into my mouth. Liang watches in astonishment as I throw the rice and juice down my throat.

"I can never unsee that," he murmurs.

"Why?" I ask with crumbs falling out of my mouth.

"I have never seen someone eat so intensely," he responds.

"What did you expect?"

Liang smiles and then glances at his watch.

"I have to go before I get late. I'll see you in a few days."
He rushes out of the cell and locks the door behind him.

"Liang? How do you get here?"

He peers over his shoulder. "Never mind."

"Liang," I say in an accusatory tone, "How do you get here?"

"I...walk."

"You walk?" I sputter.

"Yeah."

"How long does it take you?"

"About half an hour, if I walk really fast. My house is a few miles away."

"Isn't that dangerous?"

He chuckles. "No one would dare come near this place. I'm just as safe as I am in my house."

I still don't feel satisfied with that answer. "If you say so."

"Don't worry about me, Kai. I'll be fine. Watch. Everything will be fine."

But everything didn't turn out to be fine.

I clutch my head and let out a sharp breath. What was that?

'You unlocked a memory,' The Voice says.

But why this one?

The thought slams into me. This must have been Liang's room. The boy in the pictures is Liang.

A feeling nudges at me. I was there when he died but...I don't remember.

I grip the desk and a drawer flies out. A small notebook jumps out.

Dear Diary,

I slam the book shut. I look out the door, just to make sure Chen isn't watching and gently close the drawer.

I drag myself out of the room and into the next. I open the door to find papers scattered everywhere. The sheets on the bed are crumpled and the curtains are closed. Clothes are piled in the corner.

I step forward.

Crunch.

I glance behind me and bend down to pick up the envelope.

This could be a document.

My heart races at the thought. I flip the envelope over.

To Zhao.

I touch the seal and it moves. I lift open the envelope.

I killed Liang. I killed my own son.

I throw down the paper and jerk out of the room.

Chen throws me off, scrambling to Liang. He lifts the boy by his neck, his iron hands squeezing. Liang twitches and claws at his father's hands and his eyes bulge out before he goes limp. Chen jerks him and slams him into a chair, splintering it into a million pieces.

As Chen's feet come to life, I pounce on him again.

"Do you realize what kind of a father you are? Do you? You're a despicable, corrupt father to a kind-hearted son.

Your son didn't fail, you did."

Chen freezes into an ice statue as the poison spraying from my mouth empties. I let go of his crumpled shirt as he melts onto the floor. I watch as his tongue twists and turns, only slurred sounds coming out of them.

A dark figure catches my attention.

Liang.

I rush to him. "Liang. Liang. Your father's okay now. He isn't a monster, at least, not right now. You can wake up. Liang? Liang? Wake up. Liang."

I force myself out of the trance and grip my throbbing head.

Chen

Killed

Liang.

I dart out of the room and slam my room's door behind me as I jump into my bed.

"Kai, is everything alright up there?" Chen calls out from downstairs.

"Yes, Father," I respond, yelling at the top of my lungs.

But everything is not alright.

I'm living with a murderer.

A chill runs down my spine. Chen killed his own son. How is that possible? How can someone even do that?

Questions race through my mind but one thing became clear.

I need to get out of here as soon as possible.

15

ON BESH

My alarm clock turns into the sun and I shoot out of my bed. I trudge to the bathroom. Flicking the light on, I splash ice-cold water on my face. A figure in front of me does the same.

I look into the mirror and gaze into my eyes. I'm so…clean. My face is clear, not a single scratch or bruise painted on it. My hair isn't stiff and pulled out.

My hand travels to the drawer and pulls a comb out. Its teeth run through the black bush on my head, pulling it back.

I reach to touch my face. It doesn't hurt. It doesn't hurt to touch it.

I smile, tears flooding into my eyes.

I thought I would never experience this again.

Yet here I am, in a real bathroom,

When my sister isn't.

When my sister isn't allowed to wash her face.

When she's not allowed to comb her hair.

When she's not allowed to use soap.

I gulp and rub the scented soap into my hands, hard. My face turns red and my nails burn but I keep on rubbing.

I don't deserve this.

I shouldn't be here.

Bang. Bang.

"How long are you going to take?" Chen booms.

I jump at his voice and throw a towel over my face.

"Hurry up. I need to get a towel," he pounds.

"Sorry, Father."

I unlock the door to find a cranky Chen. He grumbles and digs through a cabinet, throwing everything to the ground. He grabs a gray towel and slams the door as he leaves.

I stand frozen for a few moments and then grab a toothbrush. I squirt toothpaste onto it and within seconds, my mouth is full of foam.

I cry as I brush.

I drag myself out of the bathroom and fall into my closet. Everything is so…nice. I run my hands against the cotton clothes, drops of water falling onto them.

This is all made from the cotton we picked.

From our sweat, tears and blood.

From slaves forced to work the fields.

From my people.

"Kai, you have two minutes to get down here," Chen shouts from downstairs.

"Yes, Father."

I tear a dark gray shirt and jeans off the hanger and throw them on. As I'm flying down the stairs, the itch on my skin bites into me. It's as if bugs are crawling all over.

I peer out the front door. Chen is absorbed into his phone while the car engine roars. I slip into the passenger seat.

As the trees zoom by, the clock in my mind echoes

Tick.

Tock.

Tick.

Tock.

Each second that passes by is another step closer to the pit of death.

I need to find those documents. We need to get out of here. I have to ask Chen.

"Father, yesterday, I noticed that there was an office in the building. What is that for?"

He glances at me. "It's where all camp-related things are. I'll show you what's inside after I complete some stuff, okay?"

"Thank you, Father."

The endless guard towers draw near and the metal entrance of the camp inches close. My throat closes. My heart pounds against my chest.

ThumpThumpThump.

Chen swerves the car and it comes to a stop. I struggle to keep up with him.

"Good morning, sir. We're glad to have you back," the soldiers say unanimously.

"I needed a break from you all. I don't think it's been long enough yet," Chen grumbles.

He turns to me. "Go check on the prisoners and make sure they're doing their work. Discipline them whenever you want. I'll call you after my meeting," Chen commands me.

"Yes, sir."

He leaves without saying another word. I wait a few moments before turning the opposite direction, walking through the threatening hallways. I turn left, into the factory. It's the only place that's well-lit, the ceiling soaring above everyone. The air is heavy, the lingering smell of sweat floating to my nose. Machines pant and spit out thread, workers crowding around like bees.

I wander around, peering over the prisoners' shoulders. Their backs straighten as I come close and terror fills their eyes.

They're afraid of me. They think that I'm going to hurt them.

My heart bleeds but I make it to the corner, where Hala dumps spools into boxes.

"Faster," I rebuke Hala. Her face drains of color. I lean forward. "I have to. I'm sorry. Here," I slip the phone into her hand, "I'll get it when I need it."

She nods solemnly and my bleeding heart explodes into tiny pieces. I need to make this right. I need to make everything right. I *hurt* her.

I bend down to meet her face. "I'll sneak some food for you tonight, okay?"

"Okay," she peeps and a smile buds on her face. I leave her there, a warmth spreading inside me.

The intercom above crackles alive. "Kai to my office. Kai to my office," Chen's voice calls out.

I glance back behind me but Hala is absorbed in her work.

I find Chen waiting for me. "You called for me, Father?"

"Yes. I must fulfill my promise to you. I'm a man of my word, after all."

The door opens as Chen places his ID above the scanner. The infamous scene lies ahead of me.

I gulp hard.

Chen twists his way around the countless cabinets until he reaches the farthest one.

Click.

The drawer slides forward, the key still dangling from the hole.

It's the twelfth one along the left side. Box #18.

I repeat the number again and again until it's burned into my mind.

"Come here," Chen calls. I crouch beside him, glancing into his hands.

"You can open your eyes. You're allowed to see," he says.

I take a deep breath in and force my eyes to look at the documents that could, one day, save everyone.

As the door slides back into place, my heart finally slows down. I repeat the box number in my head.

Box #18.

Box #18.

Box #18.

Chen leaves without saying a word. I back up against the wall and close my eyes.

'You're so close. You're so close to being free,' The Voice comforts.

But I should feel happy, relieved. Why does it feel like something's not right?

'You're overthinking.'

No, I don't think so. Something bad is going to happen and I'm afraid I won't be able to stop it.

"ROUND THEM UP," Chen commands as the day closes. Soldiers circle the hollow-eyed prisoners and lead them to their cells. I watch as Hala goes along with them. I catch Chen looking at me and I harden my gaze. Even I can feel the fire inside my eyes.

Chen gestures for me to come over. "Time to go home," he announces.

"Isn't it a bit…early," I respond.

"It's okay. There's only one more hour left in the shift. I just won't get paid for it."

"Ummm…Father? Can I stay?"

He looks me up and down and sighs. "I can't stop you. After all, you're going to be the supervisor one day. I'll stay for the remainder of the shift."

"Thank you, Father." I bow my head and dart toward the officer lounge. I reach into the fridge, grabbing two apples. I stuff one into my pocket and bite from the other, casually walking down the hall to Hala's cell.

Zhao sits slouched in his seat, his eyes closed and gentle snores coming out of his mouth. He flutters out of his sleep and eyes me sleepily.

I hand him the apple without saying anything and speed-walk to the corner, peering out. Zhao examines the piece of fruit, looks from side to side and walks up to my sister's cell.

"Here," he whispers and a tiny hand grabs it.

I pull my head out and smile.

16

ON ALTE

THE DRIVE HOME is quiet, the tires *screeching* below. Chen's eyes are glued to the road, his mouth curled into a frown. The smile on my face grows wider and wider by the minute.

Hala must be eating the apple right now. She must be happy.

After a few more minutes, Chen turns the car off and walks into the house, leaving me behind. I take my time, savoring the fresh air outside.

Click.

I crack open the front door to find an empty house. Upstairs, the floor screams as Chen walks around.

My stomach growls. That apple wasn't enough. I bounce to the kitchen and throw a bowl of rice and vegetables together. Within a flash, the bowl is empty.

My head begins to feel heavy and soon, the darkness overwhelms me.

The orangish-red fruit lies cut on the counter but no one is around. I open the cabinet and pull myself up on the counter. I lean forward, searching for anyone but no one is nearby.

Hala's cries erupt from the room as Mama tries to get her to sleep. Within a few minutes, her crying grows quiet.

I snatch a slice of the apple and stuff it into my mouth. A smile creeps on my face as the taste explodes on my tongue. I snatch another, and another, and another until there's only one slice left.

Soon, there's nothing left on the counter. I jump off the counter and finish my book on the couch. Gentle footsteps step out of Hala's room and Mama tip-toes back to the kitchen. When she gets here, she sighs disappointedly.

"Ürkesh?" she calls out from the kitchen.

"Yes," I respond.

"Did you eat the apple on the counter?"

"No, Mama," I respond but regret it. A black feeling squirms in my chest. I make my way to the kitchen.

"Mama?"

"Hm?"

"I...I did eat the apple. I'm sorry. I shouldn't have lied."

Fat tears well in my eyes and drip down my cheeks. Mama chuckles and picks me up off the floor. She wraps her arms around me and I rest my head on her shoulder.

"Ürkesh, I'm proud of you for admitting the truth."

I wake up with beads of sweat flowing down my face. That...that was another flashback. I remembered.

I try to calm myself down and restore my breathing but the happiness inside me surges.

I remembered.

I remembered.

I remembered.

The numbers on the clock crispen.

5:43 a.m.

I lift my head off the counter and something rustles beside me. I jerk my head to the side. A dark gray suit lies next to me.

WEAR IT

I pick up the itchy clothes and head toward the bathroom.

"GOOD. YOU listened to instructions," Chen says as I waddle to the front door.

"Of course, Father."

I try to relax my shoulders but they're held back. My limbs are stuffed into the clothes. Everything is so...itchy.

I pat my pocket instinctively.

'You hid the phone under your bed just in case,' The Voice reminds.

I sink into my seat and sigh.

"You know, that was my suit from when I was younger," Chen says, "I would like to see you *not* complaining about it."

"Yes, Father." I put on a fake smile, "May I ask why are we dressed formally?"

His lips tighten. "You'll see."

The car lurches forward as we stop in front of the camp. "I can't deal with this. You go. I can't go to work today. Here." Chen hands me his keys. "Use this whenever you need to. I'd better hear a good report from the other guards."

He unlocks my door and pushes me out. I stumble out and he races away.

Why is he in such a hurry?

I brush the dust off my suit, clip the keys to my belt and enter the camp...alone for the second time.

"Get to work everyone," I command, cringing with every word.

The other soldiers snicker. "Look at Chen junior. Thinks he's the boss."

They all erupt into laughter. One soldier among them stands up. "You have my loyalty, sir," she salutes.

I freeze. *I don't know how to deal with this.*

The man next to her stands up as well. "You have my loyalty as well, commander," the second one announces.

The other soldiers hold their laughter until one of them explodes. The loud, mocking sounds echo throughout the room and the room warps.

"It's been a few weeks into the school year, students, and it's time to elect a class monitor. Who would like to be in the election?" Mr. Gao asks.

It would be nice to be in a position of power. I can show everyone how strong I am and that I'm just as good as they are.

A few students raise their hands.

"One, two, three, four," the teacher counts, "Anyone else before I close the list?"

I hesitantly raise my hand. "Kai?"

I nod and he bends over to write my name as well. The students around me try to conceal their smiles but soon, the whole classroom erupts into laughter.

"No one is ever going to vote for you."

"You'll lose this election in a blink of an eye."

"The Bèndàn thinks he can rule over us. No wonder the government is after them."

The bell rings and everyone rushes out of the room. I stay behind until I'm the only one left.

"Mr. Gao?"

"Yes, Kai?"

"I want to withdraw from becoming the class monitor," I croak, choking back tears.

A smug smirk creeps onto his face and he crosses my name off the list without thinking twice. I remain standing there, shocked.

"Kai, I'm not sure if you heard but the bell just rang. That means that you have to go."

"Yes, sir."

I sharply gasp as I come back into reality. "Sir?" the woman asks.

"Ye...yes?"

"Are you alright?"

I glance around the room. Everyone has left.

"Where did everyone go? They were here just a minute ago."

The fear cast on their faces tells me a different story. "What...happened?" I ask.

"Forgive me for saying this, sir. You...you zoned out and your face contorted first from anguish and then to anger. Your face turned red and you clenched your teeth. Everyone stopped laughing then and ran out of the room," the woman says.

Silence.

"Would you mind if I ask a question?" I ask.

"Of course. You don't need to ask, sir," both of them say at the same time.

"Who are you both?"

"I'm Kong," the man says.

"And I'm Yan," the woman says.

"We're twins," they reveal, again, at the same time.

"And orphans," Kong continues, "We spent most of our childhood bouncing from orphanage to orphanage. There, we learned that we must respect authority no matter what—"

"You can imagine why," Yan interrupts.

"When we were in our early twenties, we decided to become soldiers, particularly in Xinjiang. Commander Chen hired us recently, about a week ago."

Both of them sit down after the brief backstory and I sit down in front of them.

"Don't let those guards get to you. They're just jealous that a young, honorable boy is in charge of them," Yan comments.

Kong nods.

"Well, I have to go now. Thank you both for your loyalty," I respond.

I wonder where their loyalty will be when they find out who I really am.

Clink. Clink.

The jingling from my side floats me out of my thoughts. I grip the keys with my sweaty hands, my task becoming crystal clear.

I need to get those documents.

17

ON YETTE

"HURRY UP," Chen yells from the parked car.

"Sorry, Father," I say as I slip into my seat.

"You'd better be," he grumbles.

He hits the accelerator and the car flies. I sink into my seat. Time slows down as we go faster and faster.

Screech.

Chen pulls on the steering wheel and the car swings to the right. I grip the door, my knuckles turning white. I close my eyes.

"You can wake up now," Chen mumbles after a few moments. I let out a tense breath, straighten my sleeve and step out of the car.

My jaw drops.

In front of me, a massive house spans as wide as my eyes can see. The walls are made of white stone while the roofs are tiled black, placed like hats. The lawn is so green, so perfect that it seems artificial.

I snap back into reality. A few steps ahead of me, Chen tugs at his sleeve and takes his jacket off. Underneath, he's wearing a white button-up shirt with silver cufflinks.

I jog to catch up with him. At the wooden double-door, two servants stand waiting.

"I'll take your jacket, sir," one of them says, holding his hand out. Chen drops his jacket into the man's arms and we enter.

The inside is just as magnificent as the outside. My feet sink into the carpet underneath my feet. Plants hang down from the ceiling, placed in delicate vases. Paintings wave at me and the air smells like cinnamon.

A servant bows. "This way, sir," he says, walking through the elaborate hallways.

He holds the door open and inside, a long table is covered with food. Small candles lay in the center, the flames dancing. Plates of meat, noodles and rice are decorated with leaves.

The servant pulls out two chairs. "You may sit here."

Chen nods and takes a seat and I follow. "Thank you," I whisper to the servant and his face...changes.

You're supposed to be Chen's son. You can't be thanking the servants.

I glance toward the servant but he seems to be focused on something else.

These mistakes can cost your life.

Creeeaaak.

From the door, an older man wearing an expensive suit walks in. His head is half white and his eyes are slightly cloudy. Two younger men follow.

Chen stands up to greet them. He bobs his head but the older man embraces him.

"Chen, my good old friend. How have you been doing?"

Chen smiles. "Pretty well. How are you?"

"Better than last time," the man turns to glare at me, "Who is that child?"

Chen waves me over. "This is Kai, my son."

The older man's eyes widen. Before he can say anything, Chen interrupts him. "I know what you're going to say, Wei. I'll explain, okay?"

Wei nods. "Sit down. We have a few minutes to catch up before everyone else arrives."

As the four men sit, their eyes remain glued to me. I glance down at my plate but their eyes drill through my head.

"Chen, do you want to give us your *explanation?*" Wei asks.

I pretend not to listen.

"Do you remember the experiment I wanted to try out the last time I visited?"

"Yes."

"He is the result of the experiment. A perfect Chinese slave. Someone who doesn't know anything except what I've told him," Chen boasts.

I glance up to find everyone staring at me and then Chen, their eyes widened in surprise. "Che...Chen, this is amazing. This is what we need, what the government needs."

The men laugh hysterically. I grip my chair.

They're crazy. They're all crazy.

A few more people file in and the noise in the room grows. Everyone is concentrated in one area, far away from me.

I bite my lips. Everyone stares at me with hatred, the fire in their eyes blazing. Even the servants do.

"Please help yourselves," Wei says and everyone digs in.

I scan each platter and it hits me.

There's meat in every dish.

"Kai, you may eat," Chen says. I hesitate for a split second. "Is everything alright?" His eyes shoot bullets at me and my mouth grows dry.

"Yes, Father."

The room goes silent. Wei leans in to whisper something into Chen's ears. His eyes stay glued onto me.

'This is a test,' The Voice says.

I dump the pork and rice onto my plate and gulp. I shove the spoon down my throat, my jaw grinding the food.

"See, I told you. There's nothing to worry about," Chen says to Wei.

For a few minutes, only the sound of chopsticks against porcelain plates can be heard. I fight back tears as I dump the food into my mouth.

Almost one. Almost done.

Wei clears his throat. "I have invited you all here to discuss an important matter. All of you know about the suppression policies we have in place. In the past few years, we have eliminated over three million *Gǒu*. We have had some problems with escapees recently. That's why we are instituting the 'shoot-to-kill' policy. The policy is exactly how it sounds. You will kill anyone who escapes or has escaped."

Wei's voice slurs and my heart begins to hammer.

Shoot-to-kill? Kill? We're all going to die. We're never going to experience anything outside the camps.

Chen's voice overpowers Wei's. "Excuse me, Wei. Kai, you are excused," he points at a servant, "You, show him where to go."

The old woman bows and waves me out of the room. I force myself not to peek back.

"This way, young sir."

She holds open a glass door and closes it behind me. Before me, a white stone floor leads to a massive pool. The blue water sparkles in the moonlight, steam floating out of it.

I dip my hands and they sink into the warm water. I keep them in there, savoring the tingling.

After a few moments, I lean back into a chair, watching the stars above me laugh.

"KAI. *KAI.* IT'S TIME to go," a rough hand rattles me awake. The figure beside me shoves me out of the chair and drags me across the stone floor.

"I don't have time for this. I should just leave you here," Chen mumbles.

My vision clears up and my head lightens. I pull out of Chen's grasp and follow him to the car.

The car ride is a blur. The road *whooshes* by and my eyes grow heavy. The forest around me vanishes into mountains of rubble.

As we fly by the camp, I can hear everyone's tears and whimpers. I can feel their cracked bones and purple skin.

I can feel everything.

The faint lights ahead creep close. Chen swerves to the left and slams on the brake, the car jerking backward.

"Out," he commands and I stumble out of the car.

Chen jams the key into the lock. "I'm not proud of how you behaved during the meeting."

"I'm sorry, Father."

"I was humiliated, completely humiliated. You acted like a baby. You are *not* a baby. You're supposed to be representing *me*. You're supposed to act strong, confident, successful. You were none of those things." His voice gets louder and louder.

"I'm sorry, Father."

"Just get out of my sight," he grumbles and heads to the cellar. Bottles *clank* down there and he stomps back up.

I dart up the stairs and collapse into the bed. It's as if I'm lying down on the clouds. I pull the blanket over me and it weighs down on me.

It feels like someone is hugging me.

It's like Mama's hugs.

"We have to make sure Ürkesh and Hala don't find out. They can't know about this. You know how Ürkesh is. He'll start to worry," Mama whispers.

I stand in the hallway, plastered to the wall. Mama is putting the dishes back while Papa leans on the counter.

"They will find out at some point. Shouldn't we be the ones to tell them first?" Papa asks.

"They're young. Ürkesh just turned ten. They shouldn't be exposed to this."

"Well, how are we supposed to shelter them from the soldiers? We can't. They go out and play with the neighborhood kids. Someone is bound to tell them something," Papa says.

"Well, when that time comes, we'll tell them then. Right now, they're too innocent to know what's out there in the world."

Papa sighs and nods.

BEEP. BEEP.

The entire room trembles with my alarm. I roll out of the warm bed and after a few minutes, trudge down the stairs. The phone weighs heavily in my pocket, bouncing up and down.

Khhhaaaa. Khhhaaa.

Chen lies on the floor, his head on the sofa. Bottles lie scattered across the carpet.

I shake him awake. "Father? It's time to go."

"Wha...Go where?" he mumbles.

"To work."

"Work?" He nods off. "Work...work...work."

I heft him up. "Come on. We have to go. You've missed too many days."

"Fine...fine."

He wobbles into the car and it zooms forward. I grip my legs, holding my breath.

Make him stop. Make him stop.

After what seems like an eternity, we make it to 'work.' The 'work' that causes my heart to sink into my stomach.

18

ON SEKKIZ

CLICK.

A still breath of air blows into my face. I slide the door shut behind me, the guards' echoing laughter creeping closer and closer. I tip-toe along the row of cabinets.

Box #6

Box #11.

Box #15.

Box #18.

I grip the ring of keys beside me and jam them into the hole, one by one.

It's not working. The keys aren't working.

Click.

The drawer slides open, rocking the room. I peer over my shoulder, the sound ringing in my ears.

I take a deep breath and grab the first file that brushes my fingers. The crisp, tan folder cracks open and the blaring black words scream at me.

Yearly report.

About half a million Uyghurs were formally sentenced to years in prison. Over three million were captured and sent to re-education camps.

Their birth rates have been cut by half and their population has decreased by over seventy percent. Full measures have been implemented to reduce the birth rate to zero.

The document slips out of my hands, fluttering to the ground.

There are hardly any of us left.

A paper shines from the corner of my eyes and it finds its way into my hands.

I drop it immediately.

Air rushes out of my lungs.

Guards beating a prisoner.

I take a deep breath, lay the documents and *snap,* the pictures are burned onto the phone, and my mind too.

I lay my hands on my knees. *That could have been me. That could have been Hala.*

Hala.

I jam the folder back into the cabinet, lock it and tip-toe back down the empty hallway.

THE PANTING OF the machines strikes my ears first. I lean against the door frame, watching everyone buzz like bees.

The Chinese are getting rich because of us. It's so unfair, so unjust. Why can't everyone see? Why can't they see reality? Why do two kids have to make them see?

From the corner, Hala's eyes meet mine and the corners of her mouth raise upward.

At least we have each other in this mess. At least we have seen each other again. At least we won't die alone.

"Sir," Kong booms. I turn toward him, "We need your advice in Hall Eight."

I nod and follow him down the hallway. He opens a metal door I haven't seen before. My ears perk up and I watch the shadows whisper in the corner.

He turns right and then right again. The hallways are now dark. The cells beside me are empty, blood splattered on every inch of the walls. A strong smell slaps my nose. It smells metallic.

It smells like...

Blood.

I clasp my hand over my nose. "You're not used to the smell of blood, are you? You'll get used to it," Kong says.

I don't think I ever will.

The world around me starts to spin.

"What's that, Papa?" I ask the man next to me.

He pushes me forward. "It's nothing, Ürkesh."

"That's a person, right?"

"Don't ask too many questions," Papa responds and when I glance at his face, it's pale like he's seen a ghost.

"Why was that person lying on the road?" I ask. Just then, the sky begins to cry.

He sighs. "People don't need an excuse to hurt other people. They won't let anything stop them. That man died just because he was in the wrong place at the wrong time. Nothing else."

"Isn't that...murder?"

"Yes, Ürkesh, but many people don't understand what the word really means."

"Shouldn't the police do something about it?"

"The police are the ones who did it," he replies solemnly.

The words punch me in the stomach. "How...why—"

We enter the front door of our apartment and Papa kneels to meet my gaze.

"These are dangerous times. There are people out there that want to hurt us just because we're different, just because we believe in something different. They want to take us away," he puts his hands on my shoulders, "But I promise that your mother and I will protect you. No one can hurt you when we're there."

He smiles sadly as Hala jumps onto his back.

But he couldn't. He couldn't protect us.

No one is able to.

"He zoned out again," Yan's words float me back to the present. I grip my head and close my eyes.

"Are you okay?" she asks.

"Yeah. I'm fine. What did you need me for?" my words trail off when the child on the floor meets my eyes.

The girl looks at me with wide eyes and they fill with tears. A huge purple splash covers the left side of her face and she lies crooked on the floor. Two guards hold her in place.

"We caught this one stealing food last night. We were commanded to punish her the next day but since Chen is not here, you must decide how she should be punished," Kong says.

"W...Where is he?"

"He left."

I can't do this. I can't. I can't. I can't.

"How much did she steal?" I ask, trying to keep my voice steady.

"A piece of bread," one of the guards holding her announces. He says it as if she stole a diamond.

"I don't think we should waste our time on such petty crimes. There are many others committing bigger crimes. We need to focus on that."

Everyone stares at me like I'm paranoid. Kong shoves his phone into my hand and I read the message in front of me.

What should we do with it, sir?

We'll deal with it tomorrow. Keep it in a separate cell. It must be punished for not following the rules.

I gulp. I can't disobey Chen. I'll get caught. I force my tears behind the dam.

"What options do we have?" I whisper.

Yan responds. "Electrocution, waterboarding, beating. Whatever you name."

I try to come up with the least painful solution but all of them are terrible.

"What about starvation?" I ask.

"That's an easy way out for the prisoners. That's why we tend not to give that as a punishment. Isolation is used for extreme crimes and this does not count as extreme," Yan comments.

I take a deep breath. I have to survive. "Waterboarding."

The guards holding the girl down smile hungrily. "Excellent choice."

I try to keep my eyes away from the girl's but it's impossible. They're everywhere. She stares at me desperately and tears leak from her eyes.

She knows that I'm a Uyghur.

She expected me to help her.

But I can't.

I can't risk my and Hala's lives. Not while we're trying to save everyone...

...right?

I bite my lip to keep myself from crying.

I'm so selfish.

I'm so weak.

I watch the girl being dragged away and her voice cracks to life.

"Please, *please, sir*. I won't do it again. My grandmother was hungry. I didn't want her to die. *Please. Please.*"

Her screams grow distant but they don't stop ringing in my ears. My heart pounds, cracking my ribs.

My veins freeze.

My eyes scream.

My mind begs,

Please don't take her away.

But I can't tell them.

I drag myself out of the cell and back to the factory. The sounds of the machines, the grunts of the workers, everything sounds like that little girl screaming, begging to be forgiven. She was just trying to help her grandmother. She didn't want to see someone she loved die.

She was punished for caring when no one else would.

Chills run down my spine. I look down towards my hands.

I can't believe I did that.

I can't believe I hurt someone who didn't deserve it.

The whispers of those around me perk my ears.

"I heard that was a test to prove whether his son was actually Han now," a soldier whispers.

His companion responds. "Yeah, Chen had to test whether he still had his rebellious tendencies in him, even if he wiped his brain."

Was torturing someone worth passing this 'test?' Is it worth trying to save a nation when I can't even speak up for a child?

I tug on my hair. I bite my tongue to keep my tears from exploding.

I made my choice and now, I have to make it worth it. I have to get those documents, if not for everyone, for that girl.

I clench my fists. We'll prove this to everyone. We will show the world how they didn't uphold their promise. We will stop the Chinese government from wiping us extinct.

DDDDEEEE. DDDDDEEE.

The piercing, sharp bell from the intercom jerks me out of my thoughts. Outside, the sky looks as if someone dumped oil on it. Light clouds travel around, blocking the white shine of the moon and stars. Guards round everyone up, locking them in their cells for the night.

I sharply exhale and drag myself out of the doorway. "I have to go before it gets too dark," I tell Kong and Yan and they both nod.

My lips are in an upside-down 'U' the whole time and it takes an immense amount of energy to take one step.

Why should I be able to walk when that girl might not be able to breathe? Why should I be allowed to go free after hurting someone? Why? Why? Why?

As the cluster of houses grows crisp, I look at Chen's house. The outdoor lights are not on and half of his car is parked on the grass.

I walk up the front steps and try the door. It's unlocked. I put my head through after cracking it open a bit.

On the couch, a foot dangles off and heavy snoring shakes the whole house. I open the door just a little bit more and squeeze through, carefully stepping on the floorboards. I peer over the sofa to find a knocked-out Chen mumbling gibberish in his sleep. Beside him, a dark brown bottle stands on the table.

He's been drinking again.

I tip-toe to the kitchen and crack open the fridge. My mouth waters at the sight of food and the beast in my stomach lurches to eat. It's been hours since anything has entered it.

A shadow covers my hands and I shut the fridge door. *I'm not allowed to eat. How dare I let myself take something from the fridge when that girl was punished for eating?*

I slap my stomach when it shrieks.

I have to let myself feel what she felt. It's not fair that I can eat and she can't.

I trudge upstairs and flop onto the bed. I fiddle with my fingers and stare at the ceiling. I let myself sink into the pillows

Don't get too comfortable here. You need to get out of here as fast as possible. The longer you stay here, the more dangerous it is.

A glimmer in the ceiling distracts me.

I don't think ceilings are supposed to shine.

I force myself out of the blanket and stick my face into the corner of the ceiling. The shine becomes more intense. I touch the wall and it's cool, like a digital screen.

It...It's a camera.

I stumble back.

Chen has put a camera in my room.

I collapse back onto the bed and try to keep my eyes away from the camera.

I can't rip it out. That would be too suspicious. All I can do is pretend I have nothing to hide so Chen doesn't get suspicious, if he isn't already.

I lift the blanket over my head and sleep with the light on.

19

ON TOQQUZ

TAP. TAP.

"Hurry up. We're going to be late," Chen booms from outside my door.

"Yes, Father."

I jump out of the bed and into the bathroom. In the mirror, a boy peers back at me. Red lines run through his eyes, dark circles shadowing underneath. His clothes are crumpled from sleeping in them.

I peel my eyes away, splashing water on my face and brushing my teeth. Straightening my shirt, I drag myself down the stairs and into the car. "I knew you wouldn't want to miss work," Chen remarks as he glances behind to reverse.

When the car rolls off the driveway, I eye the deep tracks in the fresh grass. Chen glares into the side of my head.

"You'll understand how tough it is to be a camp supervisor when you're older."

I nod, the words not coming out of my throat.

"We hope you had a relaxing day yesterday, sir," Yan says as soon as Chen and I step into the camp. Chen scowls at her and she looks down toward the ground.

Vrrrm.

A black van pulls in, guards flooding in to surround it. The doors *hiss* open and two battered men stumble out, guards pulling at their arms. Their feet shuffle on the ground as they're led into a small, white building. One of them turns toward me and my jaw drops. He looks just like Yu.

"Look, another Móguǐ. As if one wasn't enough already," all the students laugh.

"Everyone, this is Yu," Mr. Gao announces but the snickers don't stop. Yu peers down at his feet.

"Yu, go sit next to Ürkesh. That way, we can have all the Zuìfàn together," Mr. Gao commands.

Yu drags himself to the desk next to me. I wave but he doesn't respond, his eyes wet.

A few hours later, the bell rings and all the students rush out. Yu jumps at the sound and joins the wave of students.

I sit for a few seconds before leaving the room.

"Aww, are you crying? Shouldn't you be in kindergarten?" a voice mocks from inside the bathroom.

I tip-toe to the door and peer in. A group of boys creep closer to Yu, his back against the sink.

"Please. I haven't done anything to you," he whispers.

"Oh really? You haven't done anything? Why do you think we're hunting you then," the tallest boy grips Yu's shirt, "You all are trash in this country. Something we need to throw out."

The boy raises his fist but I jam myself between him and Yu. I grip the boy's hands.

"You think you can save him," the boy spits.

I bite my tongue. The boy lifts another fist but it slams into my palm. Behind me, Yu shudders.

The boy struggles in my grip. "Do something," he commands his band of friends but they stay glued to the floor. I let go and he stumbles backward. He looks toward his friends.

"You all are cowards," he turns toward me, "You're going to regret this. I'm going to tell the police. You'll never see the light of day again. Just wait, Kai. Just wait."

That's how Yu and I became friends.

But now, he's gone.

Chen turns toward Yan. "Make sure everything is going smoothly in the factory. Kai and I are going to watch the," he smiles hungrily, "Initiation."

Yan bows and disappears into the ocean of prisoners.

"Let's go," Chen says and we enter the white building. The area is divided into stations, each managed by a person in white. Chen leans against the wall as one of the new prisoners is thrown in the first station.

"Sit," a guard barks at him and the man does. A nurse in white tightly wraps a blue band around his forearm and inserts a needle. The man winces as a purplish-reddish liquid travels into a tube. The nurse rips the needle out and scribbles some things down on her clipboard.

She leads the man to a wall, where she takes his weight and height. She takes a tiny pen-like object and scans the prisoner's eyes, scribbling into a clipboard the whole time.

The nurse nods to the guard and he drags the prisoner deeper into the building. Chen follows and I tag close behind.

Why are they collecting this much information?
Click.

I shut my eyes tight as a wave of white illuminates the room. I slowly open them but it's as if I'm staring at the sun. The guard rummages through a cabinet and throws a blue jumpsuit at him.

"Put it on," he barks and the prisoner jumps.

"Isn't there somewhere I can change?"

The guard doesn't respond.

"Ummm," the prisoner mumbles nervously.

"Put it on."

"But...but...I can't change here. There...there are people," the prisoner stutters.

"Put the suit on or else I'm going to kill you," the guard commands.

The prisoner glances around and gulps. "Yes, sir."

I turn to the side as the ruffles continue.

Thwack.

The force of the blow causes my head to snap to the side.

"Put. That. Thing. On. Now," a guard orders.

I touch the side of my head where a stream drips down my face. When I bring my finger back, it's stained red.

Thwack.

The guard strikes his metal rod at me again and I fall backward. I can feel my cheeks glowing red.

"Ye...ye...yes, sir."

I come back to reality as the ruffles grow quiet. I dare to glance and find the prisoner standing in his suit, tears barely contained in his eyes.

"Let's go." The guard pushes the butt of his rifle into the man's back and he lurches forward.

"That is how a prisoner is 'initiated' into this camp and any other. We collect their data so that we can track them down, if they're ever successful in escaping," Chen says.

My tongue turns to sand. "Yes, Father."

CLICK.

I glance behind my shoulder, my breath shaking. I reach into the cabinet and pull out another folder.

I snap pictures without thinking but the big, black text laughs at me.

Surveillance Measures.

Shoot-to-Kill.

List of Significant Detainees.

Names upon names upon names.

Pictures upon pictures upon pictures.

Pictures crossed with a giant red mark.

They're dead.

I shudder as my blood turns into ice.

If only the world knew. If only they knew.

I slam the drawer, shoving the key in to lock it. I fly out of the office

And run

And run

Until I'm out of breath.

I clutch my head to stop the pounding. I painfully step forward and into the factory. Leaning against a wall, I scan the area.

I need to see Hala. I need to make sure she's okay.

I find her in her usual corner.

Her tongue slightly hangs out of her mouth as she struggles to lift a box. She grunts and a bead of sweat drips down her face as she staggers forward. After a few steps, she drops the box with a *thud* with all the others, wiping her head.

Hala notices me and smiles. I smile back but all I can see are the cuts all over her face and hands, the dirt caked on her skin and her stiff, tangled hair.

"You're not working fast enough," I bark at Hala and she flinches.

Sorry, she mouths but I'm sucked into my thoughts.

She flinched because I sound like Chen.

She thought I was Chen.

My heart cracks but I force the thought away.

I slip the phone into Hala's hand and she tucks it into her shirt.

"Am I working fast *enough,* sir?" she asks and I understand what she's trying to say.

"*Faster.* You're not done yet."

A shadow covers her eyes and she nods sadly. "Yes, sir."

20

YIGIRME

CHEN TURNS INTO the driveway, glowing in the flickering lights. I stifle a yawn and drag myself out of the car.

"Make tea," Chen commands and disappears into a hallway. I stretch my arms, stepping into the dark kitchen. I light a pot on the stove, dumping green leaves and water into it. I sit down on a chair.

Only three words hover in my mind.

Shoot

To

Kill

The sound of angry bubbles drags me off the chair. I reach upward to grab a glass.

If Hala and I don't make it, we'll be shot. We won't have a chance. How are we supposed to—

Crash.

Time slows. I lurch forward to catch the cup but it smashes against the tiles, shattering. The dust-like shards scatter, my heart scattering as well.

Thud. Thud.

Rushed footsteps stomp down the hall. "What was that?" Chen yells.

My mouth is glued shut.

"What. Was. That?"

Drops of spit fly out of his mouth. My back stiffens.

He grabs me by the shoulders and rattles me.

"Answer me."

"I...M...Dropped...Sorry..."

Crack.

A bolt of lightning strikes down on my face. I grip my throbbing cheek and glare at the beast before me. Smoke floats out of his ears and nose, the fire in his eyes blazing.

"Clean it up."

I remain frozen on the ground.

"Now."

He shoves me into the ground and his foot plants itself into my stomach. My knees turn into water and I collapse onto the ground.

"Hurry up."

I crack open a cabinet and grab the broom. He seethes as I place the shards into the dustpan. A sharp pain radiates through my hands. I glance down, watching the red flow down.

I gulp hard and shove the pain into the back of my head.

After a few minutes, Chen storms back into his room, slamming the door behind him. I throw the crimson-stained glass into the trash and shove my hands into ice-cold water.

I muffle my yelps as the water burns through my cuts.

I REACH INTO the cabinet and pull out several files. I glance behind my shoulder.

Hurry up.

I crack open the folder to stare at the bold words.

The Three-Step Plan:

1. *Assimilate those who are willing in Xinjiang, and eliminate those who are not*

2. *After assimilation within China is complete, neighboring countries will be annexed*

3. *After the realization of the Chinese dream comes the occupation of Europe*

The paper shakes in my hand.

They want to take over the whole world. It's not just us they're after, they're after everyone.

Snap.

I flip through the papers, snapping pictures without thinking. I try to look away...but I can't. I can't take my eyes off it.

Surveillance Measures.

Officer list.

Camp Blueprints.

We need to get out. We need to get out *now*.

I slam the drawer shut and speed-walk to the factory. My vision goes blurry, my breath getting shallower and shallower.

My eyes set on Hala and stay there.

Don't act suspicious.

I wander around the factory until I reach Hala's corner. I slip the phone into her hand and lean forward.

"I can't have this. Chen wants to inspect my room. Tonight," I whisper into her ear.

Her eyes glare at the device in her hands. She looks into my eyes and nods.

"GO TO SLEEP," Chen grumbles as we enter the house.

"But what about dinner?" I ask.

"*Go to sleep.* What did I just tell you?" he barks.

"Yes, Father."

I lock the beast in my stomach away and head upstairs, keeping the door open and clicking the windows unlocked.

I grab a shirt and tape it to the ceiling so the camera can't see.

It doesn't matter if he knows you blocked the camera. He'll realize you've escaped anyway. But just in case, you need to keep everything open.

I open the closet door, turn the light off and sit near the door.

Kllllaaaak.

Downstairs, a bottle is opened and Chen loudly gulps it down.

Creeeak.

The sofa screams as he collapses onto it and soon, his snores rock the whole house like an earthquake.

I wait for the sounds to become steady, grab a bag and stuff clothes into it. I dump the water bottles and snacks in. I open my door just a little bit, stepping into the smelly air of the hallway.

Bzzzzz. Bzzzzzz.

Something vibrates loudly downstairs and I flinch. I jerk back into my room, crouching behind the door.

Chen grumbles downstairs and something ruffles.

"Yes?" he mutters, clearly irritated, "*What?* I'm coming."

He gets up and comes near the stairs. I jump into my bed and pull the blanket up.

Thump. Thump.

"Kai? Kai? *Kai?*"

I put on my best sleepy face and stand on top of the stairs. I rub my eyes and yawn. "Yes, Father?"

"We need to go back to the camp. I'm needed there right now,"—he scans me—"Why haven't you changed?"

Oh no. "Uhh...you told me to go to sleep right away so I did. I didn't want to disobey you by changing my clothes," I throw out the best excuse I can think of.

He rubs his eyes. "I'm not that drunk luckily," he whispers under his breath. "Come on down. We're leaving right now."

"Okay." I bounce down the stairs, trying to hide my terror.

What's going on?

Chen starts the car and flies down the road. I grip the door handle with my life as I sink deeper and deeper into the seat. We skid to the camp and Chen jumps out of the car, me trying to catch up.

None of the guards ask for ID.

Chen walks straight into the prison and walks down the rows of cells. The detainees huddle as far from the door as they can, their eyes not blinking as they follow us down. The lights flicker on as the end of the hallway becomes clear.

He stops abruptly and glares at the figures there.

"*Zuifàn,*" he mutters, almost inaudibly.

He speeds down the hallway again, the distant figures becoming crisper and crisper.

I stop, my heels digging into the stone floor. My eyes widen and my jaw drops.

Hala.

21

YIGIRME BIR

HALA'S ARMS ARE TWISTED behind her back, the chains dropping to the ground. Her left eye is black and shut, water flowing out of it.

No

No

No

I struggle to keep the tears inside.
This can't be happening.
It can't. It can't.

Zhao stands near her, his face drained of color and his eyes hollow. He shakes his head every few seconds. His eyes meet mine and they widen for a split second.

Chen stands in front of Hala, towering over her. A muscle tightens in his jaw.

Crack.

He strikes her straight across the face. Hala's cheek turns bright red but she doesn't flinch. She looks him straight in the eye.

My blood boils.

How dare he lay a hand on my sister? How dare he hurt her?

How. Dare. He.

I creep closer to Chen, my fists clenched but a hand on my shoulder stops me. I turn around to see Yan holding me back. She raises a finger to her lips.

Panic courses through my veins. *She can't know. She can't.*

Reality sweeps over me like a wave.

Hala and I are never going to make it out of here.

The word rings in my ears.

Never.

    Never.

        Never.

"Give it to me," Chen screams, his face turning into a ripe tomato.

Hala doesn't move, her eyes still drilling into Chen's.

He can't be talking about that. He can't be.

He grabs her by the shoulders and slams her against the wall. I step forward to stop him but Yan's grip grows firmer.

Clank.

The black device clatters to the floor as Hala clutches her head. Chen bends down to pick it up. The screen smiles as he presses a button and his jaw clenches.

"Kai?"

I swallow hard. "Yes, Father."

"Keep this with you until I have time to examine it. It's evidence of her treachery," he says through gritted teeth.

"Yes, sir," I peep.

Chen grabs something from his belt and raises it above his head. The metal rod glints in the white light.

Crack.

He hits Hala on the head and she crumples to the ground.

But she doesn't say anything.

She struggles to get up but Chen puts his boot on her ankle. He pushes down and something snaps.

Hala yelps in pain and closes her eyes.

"Not so brave now, *hm?*" he presses down harder, "Don't worry. I'll make you feel so, so, so much more pain. I'm done with you, *Mógui.*"

Chen raises the rod again.

Thwack.

"I,"

Thwack.

"Am,"

Thwack.

"Going,"

Thwack.

"To,"

Thwack.

"Make,"

Thwack.

"You,"

Thwack.

"Suffer."

Thwack.

Hala's eyes twitch momentarily before closing. Her body goes limp.

No, I almost scream out but I bite my tongue down.

Chen nods to the guards and they drag her away, her legs limp.

Yan lets go of me and my legs begin to wobble. I peer down at my trembling hands. I swallow the boulder in my throat, shoving my tears back. My hand brushes the side of my pocket.

I have the phone. I still have the evidence.

"This is going to be a long night," Chen says. He lies down on Zhao's chair, pulls his hat over his eyes and begins snoring almost immediately.

The guards look at him and then me. My voice cracks. "He was drinking."

"What are our further instructions?" one of them asks.

"What?" I respond, trying to cope with the situation.

"What should we do with the girl?" he clarifies.

Let her go, I want to say but I bite my tongue. "Wait until Father wakes up. He'll know," I say, my tongue turning into poison.

They nod and follow the other guards deeper into the building.

MY EYES STAY OPEN all night. Sleep runs away from me while my heart pounds, screaming

Hala's been caught.

Hala's been caught.

Hala's been caught.

A shadow in the corner catches my eye. Yan leans against the wall, glaring at me. I pretend not to notice but she clears her throat. She gestures for me to come over.

"I know," she whispers once I get there.

I try to keep my gaze steady. "What do you know? I have nothing to hide."

She glares at me. "You know what I'm talking about. You were going to hit Chen," she grits her teeth.

The words clamp in my throat.

"It's fine. I won't tell but *only* because I'm loyal to you *and* Chen. If I hadn't pledged my loyalty to you earlier, I would have put a bullet in your head."

Yan glances toward the pistol on her belt, turns and walks away. My heart sinks into my stomach.

Thud. Thud.

Booming footsteps echo in my ears, in synchrony with my racing heart. I step into the hall as Chen stirs awake.

He stretches his arms and yawns. "What time is it?" Chen asks.

"Five in the morning, sir," the soldiers respond.

Chen stands up, instantly towering over the guards. "Where did you detain the girl?"

The men turn around and Chen follows. I remain glued to the ground. "Come on," Chen grumbles and my feet dart forward.

I keep my mouth shut and continue walking with my captors.

We turn right and another line of cells lay. We walk past

every

single

one

until we reach the end.

Hala sits tied to a chair, a cloth stuffed into her mouth and the blackness around her eye spreading.

Guilt stabs at my heart.

She looks at me, her eyes peaceful and fearless. I close my eyes to keep my tears away.

Crack.

Chen slaps her but Hala's face doesn't move. He pulls at her hair. "You are going to regret *every single* moment of your life once I'm through with you."

Hala glares at him, her eyes shooting bullets at him. Chen lurches forward and grips her neck, squeezing. I move forward but Hala shakes her head.

"No," she mouths.

I freeze in my spot.

"You dare look at me like that?" Chen screams. He drops her as her legs thrash.

The soldiers tug at the chains and Hala stumbles behind them.

We walk a few steps ahead and a stationed guard opens a door, revealing a staircase. It's pitch-black in there, like a black hole.

Creeeeeeeak.

Aaaaaah.

As the door whines open, all that tears my ears are screams.

Bloodcurdling,

Pained,

Echoing screams.

They ring in my head, replacing all of my panic with fear. Chills creep up my spine as a sudden realization dawns upon me. I've never actually seen anyone being tortured. I've hardly experienced anything.

This is where the real agony begins. This is where the guards become bloodthirsty monsters.

These are the Black Rooms.

I wheeze.

This is where the *slushing* was coming from.

My mouth goes dry.

And this is where Chen's taking Hala.

22

YIGIRME IKKI

THUD. THUD.

Jingle. Jingle.

The chains rattle as a whole group of us descend. I inch back, getting closer and close to Hala. The only thing visible are her fearful eyes.

I creep closer and closer but she shakes her head.

No, I mouth but she only shakes her head harder. As I inch closer, she shifts farther.

She shakes her head harder and my heart sinks.

I have to do something. I can't let her be punished for this.

Creeeeak.

Another soldier opens the door and we all file into the cramped area. The dim lights above flicker as we shuffle through the hall. Beside us, blocks of thick, black metal remain bolted, unspeakable things behind each door.

Chen grumbles and shoves his key into one of the doors. It shrieks open, the darkness inside ready to eat us. Chen shoves Hala into the room and steps inside.

"Only Kai may come in. I want to teach him how to deal with traitors," he growls.

I gulp, a boulder growing in my throat but I force myself to enter the room. Chen slams the door behind me and I jump, the hair on my back standing up.

Hala stands in the corner but Chen pushes her into a chair. He wraps the chains around the chair, tying her into place.

She begins mumbling something.

"O Allah, help me. O Allah, help me. I have faith that You will not let the Uyghur people die. If my death will help everyone else, I'm willing to sacrifice myself," she whispers in Uyghur.

Chen stares at her, dumbfounded.

"What are you saying?" he screams at her, spit flying onto Hala's face. She turns away slightly. "You can *only* speak Mandarin here. *You know that.* But you want to defy all orders, don't you? Don't worry. Don't you worry. There is so much more just *waiting* for you. You'll see."

He walks up to the board behind him and picks up a helmet. He examines it for a few seconds, lost in his thoughts, then slams it onto Hala's head. He fastens it under her chin and steps to the side.

A hungry grin spreads on his face and he eyes the box mounted on the wall beside him. He flips a green switch and watches as the electricity surges through the wires. It reaches the helmet and *bzzzzz*, surges through Hala's body. Her eyes shut tight and her mouth opens.

Aaaaaahhhhh.

Her high-pitched screams echo throughout the tiny room.

My heart *s*

h

r

t   *e*

t   *a*   *s*

I shut my eyes tight.

Bzzzz.

Bzzzzzz.

Click.

Chen flips the switch again and the wires die. Hala leans forward, her head bobbing but she cracks her eyes open. She breathes heavily. Chen squats to meet her eyes.

"There is so, so much more waiting for you," he cackles and turns to look at me. His eyes are wide open, pupils dilated. They're crazed, like a predator watching his prey

bleed to death. His eyes are hollow of any humanity, any compassion. There's nothing but fire in them.

"You see, Kai? You see why I hate them so much?"

I can't say anything. My mouth is like a desert and my mind is empty, like a fresh sheet of paper.

"Answer me."

I look toward Hala and she weakly nods. "Ye...yes, Father."

"Good boy. Good boy. I knew you were different when I saw you. I knew you were not like these barbarians. You had *my* blood in you. I could teach you *my* ways. Together, we are unstoppable."

He laughs maniacally. Hala makes a soft sound as she struggles against the rope and chains.

"I'm not done with you yet." Chen makes his way to her. He grabs her by the upper arm and drags her out of the room.

I follow.

Chen walks down the hall and enters another room. It's empty except for the large tank in the middle. Chen hoists Hala onto a long, wooden board and she fights back, scratching at his wrists.

But Chen overpowers her.

Chen always overpowers his victim.

And Hala accepts her fate.

He buckles the leather straps onto her wrists, ankles and forehead. He grabs a bag and dumps its contents into the tub.

Ice.

My breath leaves me.

"Bye, bye," Chen says and the board tips back slightly, dunking Hala's head into the ice-cold water.

Her cheeks inflate and turn a bright pink. Her eyes beg, beg *me*, to something, anything.

But I can't.

I'm glued to the floor.

Unable to do anything.

After what feels like hours, he lets her back up and Hala gasps for air. Her hair and shirt are soaking wet, beads of water dripping down her face.

She opens her mouth to breathe but there isn't enough time.

Chen flips the switch and Hala's back in the water. Her feet thrash in the buckles and her fingers grip the board like she's holding onto her life. He lets her back up.

And back down.

Again

And again

And again.

AND AGAIN

Until she gives up.

Bubbles rise to the surface as water rushes into her mouth. Hala's eyes close and her head goes limp. The board comes back up and Chen unbuckles her.

"We can't have her die just yet. There's so much more to do," he squeals.

I stand, dumbfounded. *How can someone enjoy this?*

But there's no time to think.

Chen drags a limp Hala on the ground, the sound burning my mind. He enters another room and dumps her onto the floor.

Hisss.

The door hisses shut behind him. I follow him into a bright room next door.

On one side, there's a huge window where I can see Hala lying on the floor. In front of the window, there's a control panel, millions of different colored buttons on it. Chen gestures for me to sit.

"This is a new room I designed. She'll be the test subject." He smirks.

"W...What does this room do, Father?" I stutter.

"Watch,"—Chen scootches his chair close to mine—"This button controls the light. See?"

He presses the button multiple times, the intensity of the light increasing each time until it goes pitch-black.

"This one controls sound." Chen presses the button and increases the pitch and volume of the sound each time.

"I'm going to try the rest out." He fiddles with the buttons.

Everything around me blurs, my eyes focused on Hala. She lays limp on the ground, her chest barely rising every few seconds. After a few minutes, she stirs awake, her eyes exploring the room.

Crrrrrk.

The speaker inside the cell cracks to life. "Looks like someone is awake. Don't worry, you won't have time to sleep for, let's see, a few days."

Hala's eyes burst and she leans against the white wall. Her breath grows shallow.

"Well, I have other things to do but I'll be back before it gets dark. I want to have some more fun before we go back home," Chen says.

Beeep.

He clicks a button.

"I've set this on auto to make sure she doesn't fall asleep while I'm gone. You can stay or come with me. It's up to you."

I want to stay with her.

"I'll stay," I mutter and the smile on Chen's face reaches his eyes.

He marches out of the room and I place my elbows on the control panel, my head resting on my hands. I watch Hala sit and do nothing, constantly looking at the window. But she doesn't seem to see me.

The window is tinted. She can't see me but I can see her.

I need to do something.

What to do?

What to do?

What to do?

There has to be something.

Anything.

A N Y T H I N G.

My mind shuts down.

SCRRREEEEECH.

I press my hands against my ears and jolt awake. Hala sits in the same position, her eyes shut tight. The light in the room becomes brighter and brighter.

She was about to go to sleep.

I watch helplessly as Hala shivers, her teeth clanking together. I reach out to touch the window.

It's like ice.

My mouth goes dry and after a few minutes, everything goes back to normal. Hala relaxes and her hands slip off her ears. She blinks a few times, rubs her arms and walks around the room.

This continues for hours, the atmosphere of the room changing frequently. Chen enters the room and flops onto the chair.

"How's it going?" he asks.

I don't respond, focusing intently on Hala.

"It seems like you were having fun. How many times did the alarm go off?"

"A-about every hour or so."

Chen rubs his hands together. "Perfect. It's a success. It's exactly what I wanted." He laughs merrily.

He coughs and regains his composure. "Time for us to go back home. We'll leave her there for the night."

I remain in my seat, eyes still glued to the window. "Come on. I know you want to watch but we also need to sleep. Tomorrow's a big day."

Chen grips my shoulder and hauls me out of the chair.

I don't have a choice.

I glance back one more time before forcing myself to leave the room.

23

YIGIRME ÜCH

SLEEP DOESN'T COME. I toss and turn but the Earth still remains balanced on my head. I force myself to turn away from the window, waiting for it to be morning.

The chains rattle as a whole group of us descend. I inch back, getting closer and close to Hala. The only thing visible are her fearful eyes.

Each agonizing moment ticks away like an hour.

Hala's not allowed to sleep, so why should I?

I jump at the sound of footprints and jerk to gaze outside. The sun is barely peeking out from its blanket. I roll out of bed, throw on a fresh pair of clothes and dash to the door.

"We're going to have some fun today," Chen announces as we get into the car.

My stomach sinks and we don't talk for the rest of the ride. I watch the trees fly by until they slow down. Chen reverses to park the car and runs out once he shuts the door. I follow and he dashes downstairs to the sleep-deprivation room.

He throws the door wide open and steps inside. Hala is sitting in the corner, her eyes barely open. Black shadows droop under her eyes and red lines crack them. Her hair is disheveled and she doesn't struggle when Chen pulls her up.

He throws her onto me and I hold her up.

"Ürkesh, I'm tired," she whispers.

Pain stabs my heart.

No. Don't call me that here. Please.

I glance at Chen nervously. "My name is Kai."

Tears flood into my eyes and I force them back.

Chen smiles and walks ahead. I follow behind.

This is my chance. We can run.

I glance around but guards swarm in behind me, Kong and Yan among them. They both glare at me with mixed looks. Their eyes are neither red nor blue.

They're gray.

"In here," Chen's voice calls from behind. I turn around to see him in a doorway to a room. I squeeze Hala's shoulder and carry her to the room.

My heart stops.

Everything is...red.

The walls are red.

The weapons on the board are red.

The chains are red.

"Lay her down here," Chen commands.

My knees begin to shake and I bite my tongue.

I can't.

I grip her arm tightly and pretend to zone out. "Kai," Chen says, tapping his foot on the ground, "Put her down here."

I force my voice to stay steady. "Yes, sir."

My heart sinks.

Chen nods at the soldiers and they fasten chains on Hala's wrists.

She lets them, her eyes still barely open.

"Let this be a lesson for all here," Chen booms, "Anyone who dares to betray their government has to suffer. This girl here is an *Pàntú* and *Xíngshì*. How dare she turn on her country? We've done so much for her, providing her with shelter, food and an education and this is how she repays us? Well, this is what happens to traitors."

Chen's pupils narrow and turn red. He steps back and whips his pistol out of his belt.

NoNoNo.

I take a half-step forward but another hand rests on my shoulder. I look back, expecting Yan, but Zhao holds me back.

Don't, he mouths, a sadness looming in his eyes.

Please. Please, I whisper but he doesn't let go.

Click.

The gun loads.

Hala looks at it, her face draining, but something washes over her face. She looks...peaceful. She stares at the gun and smiles, her face shining in the darkness.

Tetete.

N

    O

       N

         O

           N

             O

The bullets rip through Hala. She staggers back, smiles at me and collapses onto the ground.

I collapse with her.

24

YIGIRME TÖT

THE SOUND RINGS in my ear.

She's gone.

Gone.

Gone.

Gone.

...

Someone taps on my shoulder and I look up. Zhao's eyes beg me to get up and I do.

Because I have to.

I stand up to find Chen glaring at me. *"What was that?"* he snaps.

"Please—" Zhao starts but I cut him off.

"I thought I saw dirt on my shoe, Father."

I stiffen my muscles and glare at Chen. He searches through my eyes and after a minute, turns away. He exits the room along with everyone else.

The air weighs down with the heavy smell of blood, crimson dripping down the walls. My eyes lock on Hala. She floats in a spreading pool of blood but she seems so peaceful.

She's still smiling.

I crouch beside her, blinking away tears. I smile back at her.

"May Allah have mercy on you," I whisper.

'She's in a better place,' The Voice comforts me.

But it hurts. It hurts so, so much.

I heft myself up and step outside, looking upward to keep the tears inside. I rub the phone in my pocket.

Krrr.

I pull out a piece of paper.

Your passport is in my cell. Find it and go to Zhao's house.

I love you,

Hala

I smile at the note as a tear smudges the ink. I swallow and wipe my face.

I jog upstairs, straight to Hala's cell. I scan the hall and quickly rummage through the whole thing.

Where could she—

I spy a blue book sticking out from under a pot. I tear it out and inside lies a small book. I crack it open to find my picture on it.

I smile.

She really was prepared for everything. I should have been too.

A soft sound comes from the hallway and I jump. I shove the passport and cloth into my pocket and rush out of the place.

"Kai to the front of the camp," Chen calls from the intercom.

I march to the front, hiding the things in my pocket as best as possible. "We've got to get going. It's getting late and I need to drop something off at Zhao's. He left early," Chen says.

I nod.

We ride in silence. I watch the road blur past me. After a few minutes, the trees grow crisp as the car slows down in front of a modest house.

Outside, plants grow everywhere, trimmed neatly. Bright colors contrast the dark red bricks of the exterior. Vines reach up, toward the roof.

I follow Chen to the front door. He knocks and non-uniformed Zhao opens the door. He seems...older. A *lot* older.

"Yes?" he croaks.

"Your book," Chen replies and shoves a book into his brother's hands.

"Thank you."

Chen leaves without replying. As he drives, I memorize each twist and turn.

I GRAB MY BAG and tip-toe out of the room. I step carefully down the stairs, walking on the edges to avoid the creaking.

Click.

I slide the front door open and walk into the fresh, cool air. I take a deep breath, glance back at the house and make a run for it.

I tear at the chains holding me back.

I run from the house.

I run from pretending.

I run from Chen.

I walk back the path I memorized, constantly glancing behind. I fly past the trees as the moon stares.

With each step, the house grows closer and closer. I jump up the front steps and pound on the door. A light flickers on and rushed footsteps approach the door cautiously.

The door cracks open slightly and Zhao's eyes peek out. "Oh, Kai."

He opens the door.

"Zhao," I pant, out of breath, "I need to stay with you for a little."

A pained look shadows his face. "I'm sorry...what's going on?"

"Please, Zhao, please. I don't have anywhere else to stay. I still have a chance. All I need is a little while so Chen forgets. Just a few days."

"What? What do you mean?"

His eyes widen as realization floods in.

"I...I can't. If I'm caught—"

"You won't get caught," I interrupt, steel woven into my voice.

"You can't know that," he responds.

"Zhao. Let him in," a female voice says. Zhao relents and throws the front door open.

"Come on in."

I peer from side to side and step into the house. From the stairs, a woman appears. A few wrinkles are taking shape on her face. Her black hair is a little past her shoulders and a few short wisps fly onto her face.

"You must be Kai," she says.

"Yes, ma'am."

She chuckles. "Call me Huan."

Zhao clears his throat. "Huan, we can't let him stay here. It's too dangerous."

"Sit down here," Huan ignores her husband.

I hesitate.

"You can trust me. I'm not going to hurt you," she gently says but I remain glued to the ground.

'You have to trust,' The Voice says.

But I can't.

Huan gets up from the sofa and folds up the carpet, revealing a door lying on the floor. Huan cracks it open, revealing a stone staircase.

"You'll be safe in there," she says.

They could give me up to Chen. Zhao has done that before. Zhao has betrayed us.

"I don't know," I whisper.

She smiles motherly. "No one is going to tell anyone. If they do," she looks at Zhao, "they won't be part of this household."

'You have to trust,' The Voice whispers again.

I take a deep breath and step into the darkness below.

25

YIGIRME BESH

HUAN SHUTS THE TRAPDOOR, leaving me alone in the darkness. I sit down, resting my head against the wall. A few moments later, the door creaks open and a cloth bag flies down.

I scramble to it and it opens. Inside, fresh food flows out. I glare hungrily at the plethora of colors.

If only Hala got this chance.

I put down the orange in my hands and *drip,* a tear falls to the cold floor.

I begin to sob.

I sniffle and wrap my arms around my knees, bringing them close.

I'm here because she sacrificed herself.

She's gone for the second time.

"Shut. Up. Get into the car before I kill you and your sister."

The man tears Hala from me.

"Stop it," I demand.

"Make me."

"Stop it. She's coming with me."

"Take her from me. I dare you. Take her."

He dangles Hala in front of me.

All I can see is red. Red, boiling, blinding blood. The ground underneath me melts away and I soar above them all until I explode onto him. My clenched hands pound, deafening thuds echoing through the air. Bees swarm all around, their bzzzzzz tearing my mind. More and more swarm around me. They sting and sting without any mercy.

Within seconds, the man isn't underneath me anymore. Hala isn't there anymore either.

"Stop. Stop. Stop. Stop. Stop. Stop. Stop. Stopstopstopstop."

The ground is but a dark blur as the man grows closer and closer, the fire in his eyes dancing and the hot smoke rising from his nose. Until time stops and I freeze in the air, the bees blocking my path.

"Move. Move. Move!"

I shove the wave away. I flap my arms wildly against the swarm of bees but only fiery stings respond.

"Ürkesh. Ürkesh. Ürkesh. Ürkesh. Ürkesh. Ürkesh."

I wipe away my tears.

That's who he was. The guard who hated me.

He was the one who took Hala away from me the first time.

He was the one who took me back.

That was *him.*

"Please, sir."

The 'superior' lifts me off the ground.

"Now, I've finally got my hands on you. You can't escape now."

"Please, sir. I'll be out of here within a second. I won't come back and I won't bother you or any other Han person again. Please."

"You do remember the history between us, right? You are the reason I'm out here rather than in Xinjiang, hunting the rest of your people. In case you haven't realized, I serve my country faithfully. You Uyghurs are terrorists, Xíngshì. I won't let a criminal like you get away that easily."

They will stop at nothing to rip us apart. The 'superior' took Hala away from me the first time,

Bao the second time,

and Chen the third and

final time.

The anger dissolves into tears again.

I didn't even get a chance to apologize for everything.

I didn't get to apologize for not fighting back harder.

For not finding her sooner.

For hurting her.

And now, I'll never get to apologize for killing her. She died because of *me*. She's gone because of *me*. I didn't prepare enough. I wasn't careful enough. I didn't fight enough.

And now, it's too late.

I'll never see her again.

Never. Never. Never.

I'm alone.

This time, without any hope of seeing my family again.

They're all gone. Papa. Mama.

And now, Hala.

Creeeeaak.

Gentle footsteps descend the stairs. I keep my face planted into my arms. A figure grunts and sits down next to me. A heavy arm wraps around my shoulder.

"*Shh,* it's okay. It's okay," a gentle, deep voice says.

I look up at Zhao's face. His eyes are full of water, on the brink of flooding out.

"Why are you crying?" I ask.

"I could have done something. I could have stopped Chen. I knew what was happening. I knew Chen would find out but I didn't say anything. She could have been out of the country if it weren't for me. Your sister died because of me. Because I'm weak. Because I couldn't stand up to my own brother."

Tears stream gently down his face. I turn toward him.

"It's okay. What happened in the past happened. We can't do anything about it. But we can focus on the present."

"Can you forgive me?" Zhao asks.

I swallow the lump in my throat. "Of course, I forgive you."

I try to smile but it doesn't reach my eyes. Zhao wipes his tears and trudges up the stairs. Right before he closes the trapdoor, he glances back at me. I nod and the door slams shut, leaving me with the darkness.

"HALA," I SCREAM at the distant figure.

I run toward it but with each step, the figure moves miles away.

I'm so close.

Just a little bit more.

A few more steps.

I halt, my feet skidding against the raw dirt. I stand on the cliff, looking at the thick, red lake below.

It's made of blood.

The lake bubbles and the metallic smell smacks me. I squint at the distant figure, standing in the sunlight.

Hala.

"I'm coming, Hala. I'm coming," I scream, my voice echoing.

I lower myself from the edge of the cliff and start climbing down. The rock my foot was on gives way and I'm suspended in the air.

I look up at the branch that's keeping me from falling.

Crack.

Its fibers start tearing.

"Nonono. Please," I beg but it continues ripping apart.

Until it frees itself.

For a split second, I'm in the air, my heart pounding.

And then, I'm falling.

The air rushes past me and my stomach climbs into my throat.

Splash.

I sink right into the red liquid, the air knocked out of me. I struggle upward, my clothes weighing me down. I break the surface and take a deep breath before sinking back down again. I get up again and this time, Hala is right beside me.

"Help me, Hala," I croak, my voice raspy.

She looks at me with a cold expression.

Pop.

Her face falls off her neck. I scream. Her skin regrows and another face takes its spot.

Chen's.

He smiles greedily and his eyes are on fire. His hair is disheveled and his sharp teeth glint in the sunlight.

I sit motionless in the blood before he waves. Ropes shoot out from underneath and wrap around my ankles, pulling me down.

I shriek, my voice turning into bubbles. I claw at the rope but it grows tighter and tighter until I can't feel my legs anymore. I try climbing back up but I sink deeper and deeper.

The air in my lungs burns and scratches against my throat. It begs to be let out. Finally, it forces its way out, turning into oblivious bubbles.

The darkness floods in.

I gasp awake and grab my neck. I look around.

There's no red.

There's no sea.

There's no rope.

I clutch my heart and feel it beat.

Creeeak.

The door above opens up just a little. "Kai, is everything alright?" Huan asks.

"Yes."

She opens the trapdoor further and sits at the top of the steps. "It was a bad dream, right?"

I nod.

She smiles. "No one can hurt you while you're here."

"Thank you," I whisper and she leaves the room. I lay back down, my eyes still wide open. My breath is still shallow and I feel as if I'm actually drowning. Sleep evades me like a deer running from a lion.

I toss and turn on the hard floor and let the cold settle on me. I stare up at the dull ceiling, listening to the gentle whispers of the house.

I can see Hala everywhere. Her face is on the ceiling, the wall, the floor, everywhere. I close my eyes and the memory of the life crawling out of Hala haunts me.

The scene replays in my head countless times. I could have tackled Chen. I could have wrenched the gun from his hands.

I could have.

I could have.

I could have.

"Hala?" I ask.

She turns around, her skin glowing in the dark. All the cuts and bruises on her face are gone. On her head, a gray scarf is fixed tightly and she's in a long blue dress.

"What...How...When?"

She smiles at me and it lights up the sky. "I knew that I was going to be in a better place," she says.

"But—"

"*Shh,*" she says as she hugs me tightly, "Just enjoy the moment."

I hug her back tightly. "But I thought you were…dead."

"I am. You're dreaming."

"I am? Everything feels so real."

"It's not your fault," she mutters.

"But I could have—"

"No. None of this is your fault. You need to stop blaming yourself."

"But—"

"Stop with the 'buts.' What happened happened. It's fate. You can't stop fate. You have to let go, Ürkesh. You have to let go of the chains holding you back. You have to keep moving forward."

"You died because of me," I say, tears running down my face.

"No, I didn't. Stop telling yourself that," Hala breaks away, "You have to let me go."

She turns around and steps away. "No, wait. Please." I run after her.

Hala stops abruptly and I stop as well. "No, you have to move in the opposite direction. You have to free yourself from your past."

With that, she disappears, the wind carrying her away.

I gasp awake, the whiteness of my dream replaced by the black of the hideout.

Thud. Thud.

Dust gently rains down on me as heavy footsteps stomp upstairs. I look up and muffled voices grow closer and closer until they become crisp. I hug my knees tightly, holding my breath.

"You know where he is," a familiar voice booms.

My eyes bulge out. *What's Chen doing here?*

I hug myself tighter, my knuckles turning into ice.

"I don't, *Dìdì*. I have a duty to the government. I would never hide something about criminals," Zhao replies.

"I've seen the way you look at those *Yěmán rén*. You don't care about your country at all. Where is he?"

"I don't know where he is."

"I'm going to ask for the last time. *Tell. Me. Where. That. Gǒu. Is.*"

The two get closer and closer to the trapdoor. My heart pounds, slowly cracking my ribs. Chen and Zhao start a shouting match.

"I don't know. Wasn't he supposed to be brainwashed? Weren't you convinced that he was different? That he was under your control?"

"That is not your problem. Tell me where the devil is."

"One second, he's 'Kai, my son' and the next second, he's the *devil?*" Zhao yells.

"I can call him whatever I want. He's my blood, not yours. You don't have children because your useless wife can't have any," Chen spits.

"Don't you dare say anything about Huan."

"Or else what? What can you do against me? You're a failure and always have been. You were my older brother. You should have been my role model but you're weak. You let your emotions get the best of you. You have never done anything right. I, on the other hand, have been a success. Our parents were *never* proud of you. They were disgraced by you."

"You know what? I'm done with this. I'm done with being mistreated and abused. All these years, I've let you ridicule me. We're brothers, not enemies," Zhao says.

"You should have thought about that before being a failure. I have to treat you like the enemy because you are sympathetic to *them*. I've seen how you flinch when any of them gets hurt. Don't deny it. Admit it. I'm bigger, stronger and more successful than you could have ever been."

The silence settles in for a few seconds before Zhao's voice cuts through like a knife.

"It doesn't matter how tall or strong you are. The heart's size matters and you have proven that your heart isn't there."

Crack.

A sharp sound resonates through the hideout and the dust rain gets heavier for a few seconds.

"What is *wrong* with you," Huan lashes, "Slapping your own brother."

"That's it. I'm leaving this cursed house. You both don't belong here. You're part of *them*. You're part of the

Uyghurs. You both will regret it and *everything* when I come after you."

Slam.

Chen slams the door behind him and the whole house trembles. There is no movement for a few minutes.

"And he thinks that we're afraid of him. He will never go after his own family," Huan scoffs.

"He already has," Zhao replies. I can imagine his face bleached.

"But he can't hurt us. You have to be confident, Zhao. You can't let him put you down."

Zhao makes a muffled noise and *creeeaak*, their footsteps retreat somewhere else. The fresh air rushes into my lungs and my nerves cool down.

I crawl to the bag a few feet away and grab something from inside. I stuff the fruit into my mouth, savoring each and every flavor. I let the drops of juice run down my face.

My stomach growls in satisfaction and I sigh. I try to relax myself but my body remains tense. My arms and legs hurt from being ready to fight. I don't even know who I'm ready to fight.

'You're ready to fight your past. Just because you're ready to fight doesn't mean you will actually fight. You're afraid of facing your past. You're afraid of what you'll find,' The Voice says.

Maybe I am.

'You have to face your fears to live. You need to fight your past so you can enjoy the future.'

But who says that I even have a future? My whole family is...gone.

'That is for you to find out.' With that, The Voice disappears.

I open my eyes to find the trapdoor slowly cracking open. "Kai—"

"If it's alright, can you please call me Ürkesh," I interrupt in the nicest way possible.

Zhao and Huan smile. "Of course," Zhao replies, "Ürkesh, it's not safe for you here. You need to get out of the country. I've gotten in contact with some people. They'll smuggle you out of the country in the early morning."

Both of them look at me, the sadness heavy in their eyes.

"But please don't forget us," Huan mutters, "Even though you haven't spent a lot of time with us, you're still like a son. You have a special place in our hearts, just like Liang."

I smile. "I will *never* forget your kindness."

"We'll let you get some rest now," Zhao whispers and both of them close the trapdoor behind them.

I'm so close. I'm so close to being free. I can't lose hope now.

I lie down on the cold, hard floor and fiddle with my fingers. My muscles don't relax and my mind doesn't stop exploring the universe. Soon, it opens up and I plunge into a black hole.

26

YIGIRME ALTE

"ÜRKESH. ÜRKESH. GET UP." A murky figure shakes me awake.

"Huh?" I croak.

"Hurry up. You don't want to be late," Zhao says.

I jump off the floor and stuff everything into a cloth bag. I fly up the stairs, out of the hideout and stand attentively at the door.

Huan comes out of the kitchen with another bag.

"Here," she hands it to me and my arms fall down. She laughs. "There's extra food, water and clothes in there. We've also put enough money for a plane ticket. That way, money doesn't stop you from getting far, far away from here. You have your passport?"

I pat my pocket and touch the tiny book. "Yes."

A red light flashes in front of the back door.

"He's here," Zhao says as he emerges from the kitchen.

"Thank you both so much for everything. I wouldn't have been able to survive if it wasn't for your kindness. I can't thank you enough," I say.

"You would have survived. You've proved that many times." Zhao wraps his arms around Huan and me and we stand there for a few seconds.

"Hurry now. You don't want to be late," Huan pulls Zhao away.

I step out of the house and into the fresh breeze. A blue car stands in the back.

It's so...normal.

A man steps out of the car. He's short, almost until my chin.

He's Uyghur.

The man gestures for me to get in after opening the door. I glance back at Zhao and Huan in the doorway. They nod and I step into the car.

"You need to get under here," the man gestures under the pile of things in the backseats, "We can't risk anything. You have to stay there until we tell you otherwise."

We?

I glance toward the passenger seat to see an old woman. Wrinkles droop on her skin and her eyes are barely visible. A white scarf covers her head.

She looks into the mirror and smiles a toothless smile at me. I smile back.

I turn around. The man holds the carpets up and points to the gap under them.

I steel myself and lay down on the car floor.

Flop.

The carpets fall onto me and a blanket rests a few inches above my head. My whole body is put under weight and I can't move. After a few minutes, I begin to sweat and the air grows heavy and warm.

My heart wanders to every bad scenario and my heart pounds.

It's okay. No need to worry. You can trust them.

But I can't get the worry out of my head. At least, not until I'm out from under here.

"We're going to start driving now. It's not that long of a drive. About a day or so," the man says.

"Okay," I respond.

I stare up at the ceiling through a small hole in the blanket. My stomach occasionally lurches forward and back, like a rocking ship.

Thump. Thump.

'Calm down,' The Voice surfaces.

I can't. I need to get out of here. I need to get out of the country.

'There's nothing you can do to go faster. Worrying isn't going to help you.'

I try to relax as the wind whooshes past the car. My nerves cool down as if someone poured water, and my muscles calm down. My head stops racing and my heart stops pounding.

Blackness spots my vision and slowly, my mind opens up to the universe.

SCRRRRREEEECH.

The sharp, piercing sound jerks me out of my sleep. Beats of sweat drip down my face.

"It's you again. The carpet seller, right?" A heavy voice says.

"Yes, sir. Business never fails to take me out of the country. I'm assuming you have to search my car," the driver responds.

"Just a quick check to make sure. Ah, I see you have your mother with you as well."

Nonono.

He'll find me.

I'll never get out of China.

"Yes, it's always nice to have company. I thought she deserved to see the world a little."

Krrrrr.

The trunk door gently opens and plastic bags are ruffled. Someone touches the carpets and my heart stops.

"You're good to go," the guard says and the trunk door closes. My sweat turns into ice and the air rushes into my lungs.

The car roars to life.

"See? I told you we'll be okay. Do you trust me now?" the driver asks.

I hesitate. "Yes. Yes, I do."

"You're Hala's brother, right?"

The sound of her name crushes me internally. "Yes."

"How is she? Do you know? The last time I saw her, she was in Kazakhstan. She must be living peacefully now, right?"

I take a deep breath. "She...she was kidnapped and taken back to the camps." That's all I'm able to say before my voice cracks.

"Oh...is she—"

"Dead. She's dead. They killed her," I croak.

Silence.

I WAKE UP with a roaring headache. Something flashes before my eyes and I squeeze them shut. I grip a carpet, holding my breath.

They've got me. They're going to kill me.

I blink my eyes open when nothing slices my neck. I look up at the rays of warm sunlight.

The car rolls to a stop and I jerk forward slightly. The door opens, allowing the cool breeze to rush through the stuffed vehicle.

"Good, you're awake," the driver says as he piles the carpets off me. He helps me out of the trunk and I step into the parking lot.

I stumble forward as the muscles in my legs refuse to move. I hold onto the trunk, allowing them to stretch.

A smile crawls onto my face.

So this is how freedom feels. This is how it feels to be free. To be far away from the hunters.

27

YIGIRME YETTE

"YOUR JOURNEY ISN'T over," the man says, "I'll wait with you until your next ride comes."

"Thank you," I whisper and he smiles.

We lean against the car, watching the sun go to sleep. The sky turns into a murky reddish-orange.

Creeak.

A car door opens and gentle footsteps inch close. The driver's mom hobbles to the back and places herself between me and her son.

"You were in the camps, right?" she asks, her voice raspy.

I nod and push the memories away. She lifts her sleeve up just a little to show the gnarled patch of skin.

She doesn't need to tell me what happened.

"They thought they could get to me. They thought they could break my spirit but they didn't. They didn't break yours either," she searches deep into my eyes, "I can see it in your eyes. You've lost so much."

A tear drips down my face.

"But you've braved through it. You've survived. You've proved to everyone that no one can put you down."

The woman smiles sadly and I wipe my eyes. The man put a hand on his mother's shoulder and she looks back at him. "He's here," the man says.

I stare at the approaching gray car. It swerves to the left and the driver scrolls his window down.

"Ürkesh, right?" the young man asks.

I nod.

"Get in. It's time to get as far away as possible."

I nod and jerk backward, grabbing the man and his mother in an embrace. A lone tear drips down my face. "Thank you so much. Thank you. Thank you," I sob into their clothes.

The man squeezes me and lets go. I wipe my eyes. "Everyone has a part in the world. I'm just fulfilling mine. Now go fulfill yours."

I take a step forward and glance back. The man nods and I enter the vehicle. I lay down on the seat, making sure my head is under the window.

The man chuckles. "You don't have to hide here. You're free now. They can't do anything to hurt you."

I grunt and sit up, the car roaring to life.

THE MAN PULLS into the parking lot and turns back to look at me.

"For extra precaution, we're going to sleep in the car," he says.

He leans backward, pulls his hoodie over his eyes and soon, gentle snores rock the car. I lay my head against the door, my eyes fluttering shut.

"You think I can't find you?" a familiar, deep voice booms.

My eyes shoot open, my breath shallow. I look around but there's no one.

He can't get to you. He can't.

But the terror in my heart doesn't leave.

I pull my jacket over my eyes.

Thud. Thud. Thud.

I peek from underneath it at the growing shadow beside me. A shudder escapes my lips and the shadow leans into my face.

"I'm so close. So close," Chen's voice whispers.

Its claws wrap around my arm.

"Stay away from me. Stay away," I shriek at it.

"Is everything alright?" the driver asks. I turn to look at the shadow but it's gone.

"Yes. I'm sorry for waking you up," I mutter.

The man chuckles and goes back to sleep. I stay awake the whole time.

THE SUN PEEKS out of its hiding place as the car jerks awake. I remain still against the car door, my eyes dry and my head pounding.

"What do you want to eat?" the man asks.

"Hm?" I respond.

The man looks behind at me. "You didn't sleep all night, did you?"

I shake my head.

"We'll grab something to eat and then, try going to sleep."

"Okay," I whisper.

The car glides on the road for a few minutes before stopping in front of a grocery store.

"Stay here. I'll be back," the man grunts as he steps out of the car.

Click.

All the doors lock but I still don't feel safe. I hug my legs, waiting

And waiting

And waiting.

The man comes back after what seems like hours. He throws a bag in the back.

"There are a bunch of things in there. I didn't know what you would like."

The man swallows a banana whole and we set off down the road. Cars *whoosh* by and the road turns into a monotonous gray as the scene flies by outside. The sun follows us around as we pass city after city.

"MAMA? WHAT'S this place?"

I crawl into Mama's lap and crack open my book. She laughs. "That's Tokyo, Japan."

"This one?"

"London, England."

I gasp at the scene before me. "What about this one?"

"Istanbul."

I point at the picture and look up into Mama's eyes. "Can we go there? Please?"

She smiles. "We'll see. Maybe when you're a bit bigger."

"I'm big, see?" I jump off her lap and stand straight.

"Well, if you're a big boy, go brush your teeth."

I run to the bathroom and within a minute, jump back into Mama's lap. "See, I brushed my teeth. Can we please go to that place tomorrow?"

Mama was right. I would go to Turkey when I was older. She never told me I would be alone.

I stare at the city before me. The towering pillars of Hagia Sophia reach toward the sky. Birds flock together and people bustle around.

Everything is so normal.

Everyone is so normal.

They talk, play and laugh.

It's like they don't care.

They don't care about us.

They're continuing on without us.

I swallow hard and look at the driver. My voice quivers. "Are you sure this is where I'm supposed to be?"

He nods and shoves a paper into my hands. "This is where we part ways."

I glance down at the paper and touch the note attached.

Love, Zhao and Huan.

My eyes widen in shock at my destination.

The USA.

I smile and blink back tears. The man chuckles. "Now, hurry. You don't want to get late, do you?"

I scoop the man into a hug and run into the building with a small bag. I double check my pocket and rub my passport.

I'm really free.

My heart flips as I approach the counter.

28

YIGIRME SEKKIZ

"ATTENTION. WE WILL NOW begin takeoff. Please, put your seatbelts on and close the tables in front of you. Make sure your devices are on airplane mode," the speaker above me announces.

I touch my seatbelt and lurch forward. I grip the edge of the window and stare at the ground moving beneath me.

I sink into my seat.

It's okay. It's okay. The plane has to move in order to get anywhere.

Everything will be fine.

As the plane starts to speed up, I brace myself and hold my stomach. Soon, the wheels leave the ground and we're soaring above the sky. My ears pop. I clutch them.

"Here. This will help," a flight attendant hands me a piece of green gum. I look at her and then sniff it, the strong smell of mint slapping me.

"It's safe to eat. I haven't poisoned it," the attendant laughs.

If only she knew.

I pop the gum into my mouth and relax into my seat. I can finally feel my ears. I look at the white outside the window.

"I'm assuming this is your first time flying?" someone peeps from beside me. I turn to find a middle-aged man with a long trench coat smiling at me.

"Yes."

He laughs and it sparks a bit of light inside me. "I can tell because you're absorbed into the view."

He's British. His accent gives it away.

"I'm John, by the way. What's your name?"

Something wiggles inside me.

You can't trust anyone.

"I'm Kai."

"That's a nice name. Where are you from?"

My tongue grows rough. I can't tell him where I'm from. I can't.

"Mongolia."

"Ah, interesting. I've never met anyone from there. Did you enjoy Turkey?"

I nod, my heart still racing.

"Well, it's nice to meet you," he says and puts on his headphones.

CLING.

"We are going to begin landing shortly. Please put on your seatbelts and fold the stow-away tables. Everything must be put away and all electronic devices must be kept in airplane mode. Please don't get out of your seat until the sign above turns off. Thank you and we hope you had a great journey," a woman says in the speaker above.

I rub my eyes and look out the window. Buildings reach the sky, forming a grayish-black wall. It blocks the sunlight and clouds run and cover every inch of the sky.

It's *nothing* like Xinjiang.

My ears begin to pop again and I swallow every second. Soon, the plane touches the ground and we jerk forward, everything becoming still.

Everyone unclips their seatbelts and a few minutes later, stands up, grabbing their things from the overhead compartment.

I remain seated as everyone else stands in line. Soon, it begins to move forward and I wait until there's no one left.

The seats fly by as the line creeps closer and closer to the exit. At the exit, the pilot nods at me. I nod back.

As I enter the bustling airport, I notice how small I am. Every inch of the place has someone on it. People laugh, talk and walk, some holding food in their hands.

My stomach begins to grumble.

I clutch it and make my way to the first food place I see.

"Excuse me. Do you have anything...Halal?" I ask in English.

"Ürkesh, Hala. Dinner," Papa calls from the living room.

"Coming." I put down Macbeth and knock on the bathroom door.

"Hala, dinner time," I say.

"One minute, Englishman," she calls out from inside.

Click.

The door opens up and Hala steps out, her shirt wet from her hair.

"Englishman? Seriously?" I ask as we walk down the hall.

"Yes. You hardly speak to me in anything else."

"If we want to move to America, we have to be able to speak English well."

"Well, it's not like we're going there anytime soon," she replies and we sit down on the carpet.

"Sir? Sir?" the cashier waves in front of me.

"Yes? I'm sorry."

She grumbles. "What's Halal?"

"Uh…do you have anything vegetarian?" I ask.

"Fries. Would you like that?"

"Yes, please. May I have some juice with it too?"

She punches some buttons. "Of course. I'll be out with your order shortly."

She disappears behind a set of doors and after a minute, emerges with a paper bag.

"That'll be eight dollars."

I fish around in my pocket and count out eight dollars.

"Thank you," I say.

The cashier nods. "Next."

I pull out a chair. I examine the food and without thinking, throw it into my mouth.

I stop before swallowing.

What if it's poisonous? What if they're trying to kill me?

'Not everyone is out to kill you. Now eat before your stomach eats you,' The Voice rebukes.

I shove everything into my mouth. When I glance down, everything is gone, only the paper bag remaining. I get up and throw the bag into the trash.

Where am I going to go now? No one knows who I am or what I'm doing here. I don't have anywhere to go.

As I wander in my head and in the airport, I manage to find the long set of doors that will lead me to the outside world. I hesitate before pushing the door and a cold gust of wind blows through me. My teeth clatter but stop after a few seconds.

I sigh and walk to the right, not knowing where to go. Someone taps on my shoulder and I jerk back, my fists in the air.

"Relax, Ürkesh. You're safe," a woman says, *in Uyghur.*

I drop my fists and hug her tight. "Aunt Noor."

She squeezes. "I'm so glad you're alright." She looks up at me, into my eyes.

I turn away, fighting tears.

She looks just like Hala.

"You have to let me go," Hala's voice whispers in my ear. I force myself to look at Aunt Noor.

"Where is everyone else? Where's your father? Where's Hala?"

I peer down. "They're...they're—"

"I can't believe it," she whispers, "I don't believe it."

I shake my head.

"They can't be. It's not possible. Not all of them."

I look Aunt Noor in the eye. "All of them," I whisper.

I see it all again.

Papa being clubbed to death.

Mama being shot to death while Hala watches.

Hala being executed right in front of me.

I watch it all happen again.

"Ürkesh. Ürkesh. It's okay. Everything's okay. Everything's okay. Let's get you home."

Aunt Noor grips me by the shoulders and leads me to her car. I enter, my mind blank and my movements robotic.

29

YIGIRME TOQQUZ

THE CAR RIDE IS silent, the air thick with grief. The buildings roll by as the city retreats behind us. Cars *whoosh* by on the highway.

Aunt Noor turns right, entering an apartment complex. I glance at the clock.

10:38 p.m.

We've been in the car for over three hours.

Aunt Noor turns left,

Then left,

And then right,

Parking in front of building eight.

The car's doors unlock and she steps out, waiting for me.

I rub my eyes and get out of the car. The chilly air slaps me and I rub my arms. The streetlights tint the surroundings yellowish-white, the zooming cars filling the air with noise.

Aunt Noor begins to walk toward the building and I follow. We trudge up the stairs. Spiders crawl out from corners and the dead leaves *crunch* under our feet. We walk to the end of the hallway.

Apartment 824.

Click.

The door opens to a cozy apartment. The kitchen counter is made of white marble, gray streaks running through it. An island floats in the middle and a wooden desk lies in the corner beside it.

Left to the kitchen is the living room. A thin, beige carpet runs across the floor as a dark gray sofa rests upon it, a metallic table in front of it.

"You're allowed to explore," Aunt Noor says, putting her purse on the counter.

I take my shoes off and tip-toe to the room closest to me. Inside, a large mattress lays on the floor, surrounded by emptiness. From the wall, a door opens to a bathroom.

This must be the guest...my room.

I make my way to the opposite side of the apartment and peer in. A wooden bed is placed in the corner and a medium-sized TV is mounted in front of it.

Aunt Noor approaches behind me.

"I'm sorry about your room. I wasn't expecting someone so I didn't have enough time to fix it," she says.

"No, no. Don't apologize. I'm grateful for all you've done for me."

She smiles sadly. "I got an email for you."

She hands me a phone.

Dear reader,

Please get this message to Ürkesh. It is of utmost importance.

I glance at Aunt Noor and she nods. I keep reading.

Dear Ürkesh,

I know you might be confused about who I am but I knew your sister, Hala. I interviewed her (the link is below), hoping that it would be enough to convince certain countries of the Uyghur genocide. However, she was punished for it since the Chinese posted a video of her condemning everything she said.

The reason I am reaching out to you is because you can help save your nation. You can be the proof the world needs. I know you might have difficulty trusting me but please, please, consider my offer. If you accept, we can set up a video conference to discuss what we can do.

I hope to hear from you soon,

Amy Wang

"Do you want to read the article?" Aunt Noor asks.

I nod and she clicks on the link.

Re-education Camps in The Perspective of a Uyghur Girl

Hi, my name is X* and I'm a resident at a Chinese 're-education camp.' I'm kept fed, clothed and sheltered in exchange for working for the government. The Chinese teach me their ways so I may be successful in the world.

Everything I have written in the previous paragraph is a lie. That is what the Chinese government (CCP) claims. I know the reality of these 're-education camps.' They're concentration camps, where the Uyghurs are detained against their will. We're tortured, starved and killed here just because we believe we're Muslim. The Chinese force us to denounce our religion and adopt their ways because otherwise, we're 'uncivilized.'

This genocide has been going on for years yet no one is doing anything. Very few countries have stood up for us and we're on the brink of extinction. Please, please, please speak out for us. Please stop China before we're all gone.

*The victim's name is kept hidden for safety reasons

I glare at the words. My mind spins until it turns blank.

"What do you think?" Aunt Noor asks.

"I...I don't know."

"Do you want to talk with Amy?"

"I'm not sure."

"Why don't you give it a try? There's no harm in talking to her once," Aunt Noor says.

"Okay."

She nods and begins typing a response.

"ÜRKESH! I'M glad to finally meet you." A young woman beams on the screen. She's wearing a gray suit and her black hair is tied tightly in a ponytail. She looks...Han.

"Umm..."

She examines my expression. "I look Han, right? That's why you're hesitating?"

I nod.

She leans into the camera. "If your sister trusted me, then you can trust me."

I take a deep breath and turn back to the screen.

"I need information. I need irrefutable testimony so that people will take this seriously," she says, her expression hardening, "Can I interview you?"

My mouth goes dry. "I...I don't know."

She sighs and her eyes grow sad. "Can you let me know by tomorrow?"

Aunt Noor comes from behind me. "Tell her," she whispers in my ear and nudges me.

"Well...I...Does hard evidence work?" I peep.

Amy's face lights up and she nods. Aunt Noor hands me the phone and nods.

I hold up the phone and she squints to see the picture. A smile widens on her face.

"You...That's real?" she asks.

I nod. A tear streams down Amy's face. "That's exactly what we need. That's exactly what will convince everyone. We can submit that to the UN."

"Really?"

She nods. "They can stop China. They can do something about it. Can you email me those documents?"

Doubts rush into my mind.

What if...

What if...

What if...

"You need to trust me, Ürkesh. Please," Amy pleads.

I take a deep breath. "Okay. Just, please, keep me anonymous."

EPILOGUE

"ÜRKESH. CAN I COME in?" Aunt Noor knocks on the door. I peel my eyes off my book. "Yes."

She cracks open the door and glances at my book. "Amy responded."

I roll off the bed and stand beside her, peering into the screen.

Dear Ürkesh,

I hope you are doing well. I've attached a screenshot of the UN's email.

Aunt Noor clicks on the picture.

Dear Ms. Wang,

We hope to find you in the best of circumstances. We have discussed your evidence with the rest of the committee and have voted upon the issue. We're sorry to inform you that we will not debate about this issue.

Thank you for your time.

"What?" I mutter under my breath.

I look toward Aunt Noor to see her jaw hanging and her face bleached.

"After all this, after everything, they're not even going to *talk* about it."

The one entity that could have done anything has abandoned us.

Hala died for nothing.

The thought echoes in my ears.

She sacrificed herself for nothing.

I swallow the lump in my throat.

"How? How?" Aunt Noor begins to cry, tears streaming down her face. I wrap my arms around her.

We stand in silence.

"I will never forgive them. Never, ever," she whispers.

"Please don't say that."

She breaks away and her dark, tired eyes look into mine. "Why? W...Why?"

I try to smile. "Because I...forgive Chen. I forgive them all. I shouldn't hate them like they hate me."

Aunt Noor's eyes fill with tears. She smiles and squeezes my shoulder. "I'm so proud of you, Ürkesh. You've grown to be a compassionate, courageous man, just like your father."

She wipes her eyes and leaves the room. I collapse into my bed, staring up at the ceiling.

I smile as memories flood into my mind. The faces of my family float before my eyes.

Hala chuckles, her smile reaching the corner of her eyes.

Mama stands in the kitchen, calling us over for dinner.

Papa sits entranced in a newspaper, his expression changing every time he reads something interesting.

"I forgive Chen," I whisper, "I forgive Chen."

It's finally over.

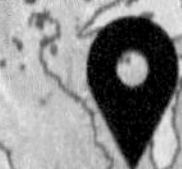

Aunt Noor's House
Chicago

Airport
Astana
Chen's Camp
Istanbul
Xinjiang
N
W
E
S

AUTHOR'S NOTE

*"The ultimate tragedy is not the oppression and cruelty by the
bad people but the silence over that by the good people"*
-Martin Luther King Jr.

There is nothing much to write here but I will say this:
the people are silent. The UN is silent. Governments are
silent. Everyone is silent. This silence has cost millions
and millions of lives.

I hope that by reading Endangered and
Abandoned, you can see how the world has failed the
Uyghurs. I hope you can see how much they have to
suffer because of everyone's silence. But it's never too
late. There's still hope as long as there are people who
speak up.

One voice can change the whole world and it's
your choice to use it.

Kian Sabik

ACKNOWLEDGEMENTS

They say the second is harder than the first. It doesn't take one, but many, to make my novels possible. I would like to thank everyone who helped make my books a reality. Special thanks to:

All of my family for your immense support and encouragement.

Mom and Dad for being the most incredible supporters throughout the whole process and for giving your opinions when I came every night.

My sister and brother for bearing with me as I bounced idea after idea onto you both, helping me with everything and reading my book before it was anywhere near the final version.

R Santamaria for being a reader, supporter, marketer and for inspiring the last line of this story. Your quotes were a constant companion throughout the writing process and beyond.

My beta readers, C Bellerose and C Yother, for reading my novel and providing feedback and suggestions. They have been incredibly valuable to this story.

My cover designer from Ebook Launch for designing the compelling cover. It's after this part that everything seemed real.

My editor, E Jane, for polishing my book with your thorough and detailed edits.

All the bookstaggramers and reviewers who spread word of Endangered and invited readers to join the characters' journey.

And last but not least, you, the reader. You are the one that makes the difference. I hope you were able to experience what Urkesh and Hala went through. Please spread the word and review Abandoned so maybe together we can save an abandoned nation.

You are the difference.

ABOUT THE AUTHOR

Kian Sabik's secluded workspace is her refuge from a complex world. Having a passion for intellectual pursuits, Kian finds comfort in reading and writing, sailing between tales of the past and present. When not drawn into a world of words, Kian loves traveling, bike riding, playing chess, sparring, and listening to her favorite podcasts. If you want to find out when Kian's next book will come out, follow her on Instagram at @kian.sabik.